The
NAUGHTIEST
GIRL
Marches On

90710 000 493 366

Have you read them all?

Enid Blyton®

The NAUGHTIEST GIRL

Marches On

WRITTEN BY ANNE DIGBY

HODDER

HODDER CHILDREN'S BOOKS

First published in Great Britain in 1999 by Hodder & Stoughton
This edition published in 2021

1 3 5 7 9 10 8 6 4 2

Enid Blyton® and Enid Blyton's signature are registered
trade marks of Hodder & Stoughton Limited
Text © 2021 Hodder & Stoughton Limited
Illustrations by Claire Powell © 2021 Hodder & Stoughton Limited

A CIP catalogue record for this book is available from the British Library.

ISBN 978 1 444 95869 0

Printed and bound in Great Britain by Clays Ltd, Elcograf S.p.A.

Typeset in Caslon by Avon DataSet Ltd, Arden Court, Alcester, Warwickshire

The paper and board used in this book are made from wood
from responsible sources.

Hodder Children's Books
An imprint of Hachette Children's Group
Part of Hodder & Stoughton
Carmelite House
50 Victoria Embankment
London EC4Y 0DZ

An Hachette UK Company
www.hachette.co.uk
www.hachettechildrens.co.uk

CONTENTS

INTRODUCTION

by Cressida Cowell

bestselling author of the
How to Train Your Dragon series

Like so many, many children before and after me, Enid Blyton's books played a crucial role in turning my nine-year-old self into a passionate reader.

That is because Enid Blyton had an extraordinary knack for writing the kind of books that children actually *want* to read, rather than the kind of books that adults think they *should* read.

Enid Blyton could tap into children's dreams, children's desires, children's wishes, with pinpoint accuracy. She knew that every child, however good and well-behaved they might look on the outside, secretly longed to be Elizabeth Allen, the naughtiest kid in the school. I'm afraid I entirely cheered Elizabeth on, as she defied her parents, the headmistresses, her schoolmates, and the very serious School Meetings. If anything, I wanted her to be even naughtier.

But *The Naughtiest Girl* books were really my favourite of Enid Blyton's school stories because of Whyteleafe, a very different school from Malory Towers or St Clare's. What if there could be a school in which discipline was administered by the children rather than the adults? In which all money was given in at the start of the term and distributed among the children along socialist lines? Wouldn't this be the kind of school that children would actually *want* to go to, rather than the kind of school that children *have* to go to?

It was an interesting proposition to a nine-year-old, and it remains an interesting proposition.

I hope you enjoy this story as much as I did when *I* was nine years old.

Cressida Cavell

CHAPTER ONE

JAKE IS GRUMPY

ELIZABETH ALLEN was enjoying life in the second form at Whyteleafe School. By early October, she could barely remember what it had felt like to be a first-former. How young the new first-formers looked now, how small for their age! Surely, she would say in amazement to her best friend Joan, *they'd* never been that small when they were first-formers? Joan would smile gently and assure her that a year ago they must have looked every bit as small.

Being a second-form monitor with Joan this term made Elizabeth feel all the more grown-up. She was delighted to be a monitor again and refused to let her friend Julian put her off her stride.

'How long will the naughtiest girl last this time?' he asked her, an amused light in his green eyes. 'One week? Two weeks? Or till half-term perhaps?'

1

'Wait and see, Julian Holland. You might get a surprise. It's exciting being a monitor. Thomas and Emma have got really good ideas. I've not the slightest intention of blotting my copybook!'

It was a long time since Elizabeth really *had* been the school's naughtiest girl, but the nickname had stuck. And how Julian loved to tease her about it!

Privately Elizabeth now considered Whyteleafe the best school in the world. She liked the way the pupils made most of the rules themselves, through the weekly Meeting, which was a kind of school parliament. And she loved the monitors' get-togethers that Thomas and Emma, the new head boy and girl, had introduced. All twelve monitors now met Thomas and Emma once a week for tea and biscuits in their study. They helped to plan the main Meeting and were encouraged to put forward ideas. It was known simply as the Monitors' Meeting, or MM for short.

'Don't forget we've got an MM before tea, Elizabeth!' Joan reminded her friend one day.

They were still outside, after games. Elizabeth was loitering near the main hockey pitch, where members of the school's first eleven were having a team practice. There were some important matches coming up soon.

'I know, Joan,' replied Elizabeth. 'I'm looking forward to it. Wasn't it good last week?'

There had been three MMs so far and Elizabeth had enjoyed each one. She wanted to play her full part in the smooth running of the school. She was determined to be a dynamic and successful monitor. She took her responsibilities to heart.

'But we haven't got time just to stand around,' Joan said softly. 'We've got to wash and change and smarten up . . .'

'I'm not just standing around, Joan!' Elizabeth pointed out patiently. 'I'm looking at Jake and his poor ankle, that's all. I'm worried about him, aren't you? We *are* his monitors after all. I think the least we can do is go over and have a few words with him. He looks so grumpy! Come on, let's try and cheer him up.'

Only then did Joan realise that her friend was gazing not at the team practice but at a forlorn figure sitting on the grass, with his ankle heavily strapped. Joan knew Jake well. He had been in the second form even longer than she had. He was a big, strapping boy for his age. He was a brilliant hockey player and at the end of last season had been selected for the school's first hockey team. He was the youngest pupil ever to have made it into the first eleven. He had played superbly.

'Poor Jake!' she agreed. 'All right then. But we'd better not talk to him for too long.'

Elizabeth was already striding ahead.

3

It was sad to see the big boy sitting there, staring miserably into space, while his teammates practised running and passing and shooting goals. He had returned to school from the summer holidays a different boy, thought Joan. It seemed he had fallen badly on the last day of the holidays and injured his ankle. It had been strapped up for nearly a month now and he was still limping heavily. The injury seemed to have affected his confidence too. He was much quieter this term than Joan had ever known him.

'Cheer up, Jake!' Elizabeth was telling him, with her bright, friendly smile. 'We just want you to know how proud we are to have a second-former who's already in the first hockey team. And already a star! It's such an honour for us. It won't be long now before that ankle of yours is better and it won't be a moment too soon! Mr Warlow says there are some very important matches coming up and the team's not the same without you. We can't wait to see you in action again, I can tell you. The whole second form will be cheering you on from the sidelines!'

Even at the best of times, Jake was the strong, silent sort of boy. He seemed taken aback by such effusiveness. His cheeks turned red.

'Oh, leave off, Elizabeth,' he said grumpily.

'Don't be embarrassed, Jake!' said Joan tactfully. 'We

just want you to know that our thoughts are with you. It's such a shame for you, not being able to play games. We do hope the ankle will be better soon.'

'Thanks, Joan,' mumbled the big boy.

'It's got to be!' declared Elizabeth in her boisterous way. 'I am going to wish and wish and *wish* your ankle to get better, Jake! Just you wait and see!'

The boy shrugged and made no response.

'Come on, Elizabeth. We must dash now!' Joan tugged at Elizabeth's arm. 'We mustn't be late for the MM!'

As they went indoors, Elizabeth sighed. She'd hoped to cheer Jake up, but instead she seemed to have made him grumpier than ever!

'He seemed surprised at my coming over and talking to him,' she frowned. 'I got the impression that he'd quite forgotten I'm one of his monitors this term.'

'He probably had,' laughed Joan.

'Do you think it would be a good idea if all monitors had a special armband?' continued Elizabeth. 'Shall we bring it up at the MM and see what Thomas and Emma say?'

'Don't be hasty, Elizabeth,' replied Joan. 'We can't bring ideas up just to please ourselves. We go to the MM as representatives of form two. We'd need to find out what lots of other people in the form think about it first – and there isn't time.'

'Here come Kathleen and Jenny!' exclaimed Elizabeth. 'We can ask them what they think while we're getting ready.'

The four girls shared Dormitory Fourteen, a big, sunny room on the first floor. As Elizabeth and Joan prepared to go to the Monitors' Meeting, they talked to the other two about the armband idea.

'Do you think we really need monitors to have an armband?' said Kathleen, her cheeks rosier than ever after an hour on the games field. 'Everybody knows who they are.'

'I'm not sure they always do,' pouted Elizabeth.

'It's a good idea in some ways,' reflected Jenny. 'But it would mean the school having to spend money to get them made. The Beauty and the Beast might think it's a waste of money!'

Miss Belle and Miss Best were the joint headmistresses. They weren't greatly in favour of unnecessary fripperies and frills.

'We could make our own,' suggested Elizabeth.

By the time she had finished chattering and brushing her hair and (at Joan's suggestion) sponging a jam mark off her school skirt, it was getting late. The two friends hurried off along the corridor to go to the meeting – and bumped straight into Julian.

He had come looking for Elizabeth. He was still wearing his tracksuit after games and was disappointed to see her looking so smartly dressed.

'Oh, why have you changed, Elizabeth? We were planning to go for a pony ride before tea!'

Elizabeth's hand flew to her mouth.

'Oh, Julian, sorry! How awful of me. I forgot I had an MM today. Can we go for a ride tomorrow instead? But listen, there's an idea I want to tell you about. I need to know your opinion . . .'

At that moment two other second-form boys appeared.

'Harry . . . Martin . . . I need your opinions as well.'

Elizabeth stood there in the corridor and declaimed her idea about the special armbands for school monitors. Joan looked anxiously at her watch.

'Well, Julian, what do you think?' ended Elizabeth.

Her friend threw back his head and roared with laughter.

'What a horrible idea, Elizabeth! Do you want to be mistaken for a member of the secret police or something?'

Harry and Martin started tittering. Elizabeth . . . armband . . . secret police. What a joke!

'All right, all right. I was only asking!' protested Elizabeth.

She suddenly went off the idea herself. It had fallen flat. All the fizz had gone out of it. Although

7

she hated being teased by Julian, she always valued his opinion. By the time the two girls had reached the door of Thomas and Emma's big study her mind was made up.

'I don't think we'd better say anything about the armband idea, Joan,' whispered Elizabeth. 'It doesn't seem to have a lot of support.'

Joan murmured her agreement.

Privately, she was thinking about Jake. It might have slipped the big boy's mind that Elizabeth was one of his monitors, but how could he have escaped the fact? Elizabeth was so keen! She was so determined to be a successful and dynamic monitor. There was really no need for her to think about wearing an armband!

It was much more likely, reasoned Joan, that the boy was upset at being reminded about his injury, by a monitor or anybody else, no matter how kindly meant. It only made him grumpier. Elizabeth had better go easy in that quarter, she thought.

Out loud, she simply said, 'I expect there will be a lot of other things to talk about.'

'Yes!' replied Elizabeth eagerly. 'I wonder what Thomas and Emma have got in store for us to discuss this week? I expect it will be something interesting!'

CHAPTER TWO

THOMAS AND EMMA
AIR A NEW IDEA

'HELLO, ELIZABETH! Hello, Joan!' The head girl ushered them in with a smile. 'You'd better grab your tea and biscuits before you sit down. We're all crammed together like sardines as usual.'

'Sorry we're a bit late, Emma!' apologised Elizabeth.

The study was packed. The two friends had to squeeze past all the other boys and girls to get to the table where their mugs of tea awaited them. The mugs stood next to a plate of biscuits. Elizabeth chose her biscuits with care – a shortbread and a chocolate digestive.

'If you can *find* anywhere to sit down!' laughed Thomas. The tall fair-haired boy was standing by the window, waiting to start. 'Last to arrive had better sit on the floor if they can't find anywhere else!'

Joan managed to find a perch on the arm of a chintz-covered armchair normally reserved for visitors.

9

Then Donald stood up and insisted on giving Elizabeth his place on a wooden bench that had been brought in.

'I'll sit on the floor next to Peter,' smiled the older boy. 'I don't mind at all. Budge up a bit, Peter.'

Peter was the youngest there. He had gone up from the junior class to the first form this term and had been made a monitor.

Elizabeth sandwiched herself on to the bench between Eileen and Richard, who were also monitors now. What fun these get-togethers were, she decided. She sipped her tea slowly and gazed round the room. All twelve monitors had turned up, as in previous weeks.

Whereas the main Meeting in the school hall each week was a formal affair, these little MMs were just the reverse, everybody squashed into a small space, the atmosphere relaxed and jolly.

'Thank you all for coming!' began Thomas. 'I see we've got a full house as usual. And that's good because Emma and I want to give something an airing. It's a completely new idea. We need to know whether you like it yourselves – and whether you think your classmates would approve. Emma, you explain the thinking behind it.'

Emma finished her tea, placed the cup down and swung round in her chair to face them all.

'Tom and I were talking the other day about how

we all like to win honours. It's part of human nature. If we're good at games, we try to get into the teams. And, if we're good at lessons, we try to come top in class. However, some boys and girls are not especially good at games or brainy either, but they may have other fine qualities. We thought, is there a way *they* can be given recognition at Whyteleafe too? Some honour they can compete for on equal terms? What do you think?'

The monitors received the idea with enthusiasm.

'You mean, people who do something unselfish?' asked young Peter.

'A noble deed?' exclaimed Elizabeth eagerly.

'An act of bravery?' suggested Donald.

'Exactly!' said Emma, pleased to see how quickly the monitors were warming to the idea. 'All of those things. Hands up all of you who think such a prize would be popular with the boys and girls in your form.'

At once every hand in the room shot up. Thomas smiled as he looked round at the forest of hands.

'Good!' he said. 'In that case Emma and I would like to announce the plan at this week's Meeting. Let's work out the details. How often should we give out the honour? Perhaps once a term, do you think?'

'Yes! And keep it separate, so award it at half-term!' suggested Eileen.

'But what will the honour be called, Thomas?' asked Donald.

'Now there's a good question,' smiled Thomas. 'Let's put our thinking caps on.'

After that the discussion raged for several minutes. Elizabeth was aglow. She liked the head boy and girl's idea. Now they were all being asked to think of the name for the new honour. It was so exciting to be in at the very beginning of things like this. A new tradition at Whyteleafe School . . .

Suggested names for the honour came thick and fast.

'The Bravery Award!'

'The Gold Star for Good Conduct!'

'No – the Gold Star for Courage . . .'

'What about the Good Deed Award?'

In the end it was one of the fourth-form monitors, Eric, who came up with the best name. He was a thoughtful, learned-looking boy. He got to his feet, adjusted his glasses and cleared his throat.

'May I say something? I'll never forget some of the things that William and Rita told us about courage at camp last term. They knew the true meaning of courage, didn't they? And they explained it so well. I'm sure the whole school would wish to remember them.'

'They were the finest head boy and girl that any school could hope for,' said Thomas humbly. 'Emma and I are going to have to work hard to live up to their example.'

Emma nodded, her eyes misting over.

'And so, Eric?' she asked.

Before Eric could reply, Elizabeth suddenly guessed what he was going to say. A thrill ran through her and she clapped her hands. She couldn't stop herself shouting it out loud.

'The William and Rita Award!' she cried. 'That's what you're going to say, isn't it, Eric?'

'Yes! That's it exactly. You've taken the words right out of my mouth, Elizabeth!'

There were surprised gasps all around and then everyone began to cheer. The William and Rita Award. Excellent!

Thomas and Emma looked at each other in delight.

'That's a lovely name for the honour, Eric,' smiled Emma. 'Quite brilliant.'

'Perfect!' exclaimed Thomas.

And the whole room agreed.

It turned into a long session after that. There was so much to discuss! But it was all very fruitful. By the end of the session, not only had the name of the award been decided, but so had all the details of how the winner would be selected. These would be announced in full at the School Meeting.

'Until then this is all hush-hush,' Emma reminded them. She placed a finger to her lips. 'Not a word to anyone. We don't want this leaking out in dribs and drabs. It must be announced in the proper way when the whole school is assembled.'

Elizabeth and Joan were used to this. Things that the monitors discussed at MMs often had to remain confidential, until the head boy and girl were ready to make them public.

'It's so lucky that we're friends, Joan!' remarked Elizabeth, as they went into the dining hall for tea. 'We can talk to each other as much as we like about things that are said at the MMs. I'd die if I couldn't talk to somebody about them! I wonder who'll get the first William and Rita Award? I wonder if it will be anyone in our form? Wouldn't that be an honour!'

She was still bubbling over with it all when she sat down for tea. Julian had saved her a place by the window, at one of the second-form tables.

'Hello, Elizabeth!' Julian wore his usual grin. 'How did the meeting of the secret police go then? What are you looking so excited about? Did you decide anything interesting?'

'As a matter of fact, we did,' Elizabeth blurted out.

'What then?'

'It'll be announced at the School Meeting,' said

Elizabeth. 'But my lips are sealed till then. Oh, sorry, Julian. I shouldn't have said anything, should I?'

A look of annoyance had crossed her friend's face.

'It's not *my* fault,' she added. 'It's a rule!'

'Since when has the naughtiest girl worried her head about rules?' asked Julian waspishly. 'If this monitor business is going to turn you into the school goody-goody, I will feel very badly let down, Elizabeth Allen.'

'Sorry, Julian,' Elizabeth repeated.

Then he gave her hair a friendly tweak and smiled.

'Only joking,' he said airily. 'No leaks allowed from the Cabinet Office, eh? Has to be announced at the full sitting of Parliament? Fair enough.'

Daniel Carter, sitting opposite, was looking solemn.

'Julian, Elizabeth would love to tell you what happened. You can see that just by looking at her face! I'm sure she *would* if she could. Gosh, I can't wait for the Meeting, to hear what it is. I wish I'd been at the MM, Elizabeth. They *do* sound fun.'

The wistful expression on Daniel's face gave Elizabeth a sudden pang.

For the first few days of term Daniel had been appointed as a form monitor in Elizabeth's place, while she had been in disgrace about something. But, as soon as Elizabeth had been vindicated, the boy had, of course, stood down to enable her to have her monitorship back. Poor Daniel!

But, before Elizabeth could brood about it, another boy called down the table to her. It was Julian's cousin, Patrick. The two cousins liked to keep their distance as they did not get on particularly well.

'Please stop gabbing, Elizabeth, and pass the bread rolls up this end! I'm starving! I've been practising my ping-pong for the last hour!'

Elizabeth smiled and passed the bread basket along the table. Patrick smiled back.

'Don't forget it's squad practice tomorrow,' he reminded her. 'I'm going to beat you for a change!'

They were both in the school table-tennis squad, but Patrick was only the team's first reserve. He was a very competitive boy and was striving with all his might to become a full team member, like Elizabeth.

'You *wish*, Patrick!' Elizabeth called back cheerfully.

After that she tucked into her tea with gusto.

She gave no further thought to Daniel's comments, nor Julian's. It would be some days before she would have good reason to recall them.

CHAPTER THREE

ELIZABETH HEARS ABOUT A BRAVE DEED

THE TABLE-TENNIS practice, the one that Patrick had mentioned, took place after lessons the following day. Mr Warlow, the sports master, had asked all team members and team reserves to attend. He and Emma, who was table-tennis captain, wanted to check that everyone was in good form for a match on Saturday. It would be an away match against Hickling Green School, their old rivals, to take place alongside a hockey fixture. Hickling Green had a very strong hockey eleven. Mr Warlow feared that Whyteleafe might do badly in the hockey match, especially with Jake out of the team. But he had high hopes of his table-tennis squad! It was a good one this term.

Elizabeth would not have been allowed to miss the practice, even if she'd wanted to. And, of course, she would not have dreamt of missing it. She was looking forward to the trip on Saturday. Miss Belle and Miss Best had hired a full-size coach to accommodate both teams and their supporters. It would be so exciting if they could beat their old rivals, thought Elizabeth, and they would be sure to get a lovely tea afterwards.

However, it was a great disappointment to have to put off going riding with Julian for the second day running.

'Don't worry, Elizabeth. It's not your fault,' he said good-humouredly. 'It's just a pity we're not allowed to go riding after tea this term, with the evenings drawing in. I'll fix up a ride with Robert instead.'

'Let's go and feed the ponies after tea. At least we're allowed to do that!' suggested Elizabeth. 'I haven't seen them for days and I'm missing them.'

'Good!' said Julian. 'I like that idea. Off you go to your ping-pong then. Don't wear yourself out. See you at tea!'

It was a busy practice session. Emma and Mr Warlow spent most of the time coaching the boys and girls. They were shown how to improve their footwork, as well as their batting technique. They were then split up to play a proper practice game, paired according to ability. Elizabeth was asked to play against Patrick. The two were evenly matched although Elizabeth was considered to have the edge.

ELIZABETH HEARS ABOUT A BRAVE DEED

She usually beat Patrick. But today he was determined to reverse that situation. He had been working on his game furiously, for days.

And he knew that both Emma and the teacher were keeping a watchful eye on all three tables, checking everybody's current form. It made him very focused.

But Elizabeth was equally aware that they were being kept an eye on. And she was very focused too.

They both played exceptionally well.

Patrick served first and took the lead, 3–2. Then Elizabeth served and lost only one of her service points to lead 6–4. After that the lead passed from one to the other, backwards and forwards, the scores tending to go with service. The rallies were long, fast and furious.

The score reached 20–20!

Now they had to change service on every point. The first to lead by two clear points would win the game. In the tension of the moment Patrick's service faltered. It twice missed the table and he lost the point: 21–20 to Elizabeth. Then Elizabeth did a safe, medium-paced service, nothing fancy. Patrick returned to her backhand. She gave back a spinning lob that just caught the edge of the table. Patrick had to swoop low and only just managed to return it.

It was a weak, loopy return. It bounced high on Elizabeth's side of the table. She changed to forehand grip, swung her arm back and then—

Whooosh!

A beautiful forehand smash to the far corner! Patrick dived . . . too late. He missed.

'Twenty-two–Twenty!' Elizabeth cried in delight. 'I've won! I've won!'

The ping-pong ball hit the far wall and came rolling slowly back towards Patrick's foot. In his fury and frustration, and in the heat of the moment, he stamped on it.

Crunch! The ping-pong ball was flattened.

The sudden sound made Emma glance round.

'Oh, Patrick, you clumsy boy! You've trodden on the ball!'

Already regretting his temper, Patrick stared at Elizabeth imploringly. He was silently begging her not to give him away! She was the only person who had seen him deliberately stamp on the ball.

Emma was scooping the poor ball up from the floor, examining it.

'It's past repair, I'm afraid,' she said.

'Oh, what a shame,' said Elizabeth innocently.

'I'll replace it, Emma,' Patrick said quickly. 'I'll go to the village and buy a new one with my own money. I'll go straight away if you like. Has the session ended now?'

'Oh, Patrick, you are a good sport,' said Emma. 'Will you really? As a matter of fact, we're getting rather low on balls at the moment. Would you like to go with him, please, Elizabeth? You've both got some time before tea.'

At Whyteleafe School pupils were allowed to go down to the village. But it was a strict rule that they went out in pairs and not on their own.

'The sun's coming out!' said Elizabeth cheerfully. 'I'll be glad of a walk to the village.'

As the boy and girl strolled out through the school gates and along the quiet road to the village, Patrick looked sullen and shamefaced.

'Thanks for not giving me away, Elizabeth,' he said.

Elizabeth felt slightly sorry for him.

'Cheer up,' she said. 'I've got an awfully hot temper myself, so I know just what it's like to lose it!'

Patrick did not reply. The fact was that, in spite of their occasional clashes, he could not help liking and admiring Elizabeth. He often wished that she would like and admire *him*. It was annoying the way she seemed so much to prefer his cousin Julian. And now he felt angry with himself for losing his temper like that. It had been childish.

'It's all right for you to lose your temper, Elizabeth,' he said. 'You're only a girl.'

Elizabeth couldn't help smiling to herself. It was a typical Patrick remark – and just one of the reasons why she much preferred his cousin Julian!

Patrick did not speak again until they reached the shop.

'The truth is, Elizabeth,' he confessed, as they stared in the shop window, 'that I really thought I might beat you today. You've been so busy with this monitor business. You haven't been practising so much lately. I was so hoping that they'd notice me. How well I was playing . . . Then maybe I'd get a chance to play in a match soon.'

'You *were* playing well, Patrick,' said Elizabeth truthfully. 'And the game could easily have gone the other way. And I'm sure they did notice you and that you'll be given a chance sooner or later.'

A little bell on the shop door tinkled softly as they pushed it open and went inside. It was a lovely, old-fashioned shop with a warm, musky smell. The table-tennis balls were in a cardboard box, jammed between the shuttlecocks and the birthday cards.

Patrick picked out a shiny new white ping-pong ball, took it to the counter and paid for it. Elizabeth followed him out of the shop.

They stood outside on the pavement, wondering whether there was time to go across to the sweet shop, on the opposite side of the road. They decided there was not.

Then suddenly a car squealed to a halt in front of them and a mother burst out of the car, with a small red-headed child. They seemed to be in a great state of excitement. They were looking this way.

Something strange was going on.

The little girl was pointing at Patrick! She was whispering to her mother. Her eyes were very big and round. Her cheeks had gone very pink.

'Are you *sure*, Sandra?' the woman kept asking. 'Are you really sure it was him?'

'Yes, Mummy. It was, it was, it was!'

'Look at his face. You are quite sure?'

'Sure as sure can be, Mummy!' squeaked the child, getting more excited by the minute. 'Cross my heart. It was him!'

Then an extraordinary thing happened. To Elizabeth's amazement, the woman ran up to Patrick and embraced him! There were tears of emotion in her eyes.

'Thank you!' she exclaimed. 'Thank you for saving my little Sandra's life! Every day when we come to the shops, I tell Sandra to look out for you, in case she should see you again. We so wanted to be able to thank you!'

Patrick stood there, blushing. And then the woman

picked the child up and thrust her at Patrick.

'Give the young man a kiss, Sandra. Tell him you're sorry for being such a silly girl and giving us all a fright. Say thank you nicely.'

Patrick's blushing increased tenfold as the little girl planted a kiss on his cheek and lisped her thank-yous.

The woman then set the child down on the pavement and turned to speak to Elizabeth.

'I don't suppose your friend's ever told you he's a hero?'

'No!' exclaimed Elizabeth. 'Whatever happened?'

'My Sandra ran out of this shop last week when my back was turned!' the woman explained. 'She ran across the road to go to the sweet shop. That's what happened! And your friend here—' The woman patted Patrick's arm, overcome with emotion. 'There was this car, you see,' she gulped. 'It came speeding round the bend. It didn't see my Sandra. And your friend – he was so brave. He ran into the road and pushed her out of the way, just in time! And he could have been killed himself. And he didn't even stop to let anybody thank him. He just ran off.'

'Patrick!' gasped Elizabeth.

Politely, Patrick bowed to both the mother and child. Then he backed away. 'I'm afraid we're in a bit of a hurry!' he said. 'Come on, Elizabeth.'

He took her arm and marched her swiftly away. Elizabeth could sense the boy's embarrassment. He would never have dreamt, she thought, that his brave deed might come out in this unexpected way. He was walking so fast, he was almost running!

'Thank you again,' the woman called out. 'I just had to stop the car when Sandra saw you. I didn't mean to embarrass you! You're a real hero, young man. I'll never forget you as long as I live!'

Worried that the woman would take Patrick's discomfiture for rudeness, Elizabeth looked back and gave mother and daughter a friendly wave. Elizabeth's face was flushed with excitement. Her eyes were shining. 'Think nothing of it!' she called. 'It was a pleasure.'

And, as soon as she and Patrick had gone a safe distance, she jerked at his arm and made him halt.

'Patrick! I am absolutely amazed!' she said, gazing at him. 'What a wonderful surprise! I know it's a horrid thing to say, but I had no idea that you could be such a brave person. I'm really ashamed of myself now. What a fine thing to do! And to think that when it happened you didn't even wait to be thanked!'

She gazed at him, wide-eyed. She was seeing him in a completely new light. 'Oh, Patrick. I do admire you for this.'

He lowered his gaze, crimson with pleasure.

'Lot of fuss about nothing,' he muttered.

They walked on in silence, each wrapped in their own thoughts. Patrick glanced at Elizabeth from time to time, as they wandered along. Her lips were parted and there was still that thrilled expression on her face.

She was thinking about the William and Rita Award! Surely, now, no other candidate could possibly match Patrick's claim to it? It was almost as though the very award itself had been designed with Patrick's deed in mind. What an honour for the second form if the very first William and Rita Award came their way!

'What are you thinking about, Elizabeth?' asked Patrick at length. 'Why are you so quiet?'

They were turning in through the school gates. They could hear a distant bell ringing for tea.

'I'm still thinking about your brave deed, of course. And Patrick, I can't explain yet – but there's a reason why the whole school is going to need to know about it soon!'

'WHAT?' exclaimed Patrick. He pulled her to a stop and gripped her arm.

'Don't you dare, Elizabeth! Nobody's to know about this. No one, you understand? You're to promise me at once that you will never say a word to anyone!'

Elizabeth looked at him in dismay. She pouted. 'Why not, Patrick? Whyever not? Quite apart from this

– er – special thing, it's right that people should know! I'd like *everybody* to know what you're really like. What a good, brave person you are. And how you've never once showed off about what you did.'

Patrick flushed, basking in Elizabeth's praise.

'Why must I keep it secret, Patrick?' Elizabeth repeated.

The boy thought long and hard, staring at the ground. When he replied, the words were carefully chosen.

'Look at it this way,' he said. 'If a boy in a Whyteleafe uniform was down in the village one day, and performed a brave action, why would nobody know about it? At least one other person should know about it, shouldn't they? I'm not admitting anything and certainly not to a monitor, but isn't there a rule at Whyteleafe School? Isn't there a very strict rule that must never be broken?'

'Oh!' gasped Elizabeth. 'Of course! You went down to the village on your own, Patrick! That's it, isn't it? You didn't pair up with somebody else, the way you're supposed to.'

Patrick did not reply. Instead he let go of Elizabeth's arm and strode on up the school drive.

He looked back over his shoulder. 'Come on, Elizabeth. You're going to be late for tea.'

She hurried after him. She was thinking things over

carefully. She caught up with him, outside the doors of the dining hall.

'Patrick, I can see you're in an awkward situation. But believe me, I'm sure this boy would be forgiven, just this once, for breaking an important school rule. Once everybody knew what a hero he'd been.'

'He's not interested in being a hero, Elizabeth, and that's final. A hero to you, if you like. I don't mind that. But nobody else. So now please shut up about it.'

Swallowing her deep disappointment, Elizabeth went in to tea. Julian and Joan were wondering where she'd got to. Julian's eyebrows rose high upon seeing her enter the dining hall with Patrick.

They explained how they'd gone down to the shops to buy the new ping-pong ball. Patrick whistled cheerfully and bounced it on the table a few times. Elizabeth watched admiringly.

Later, when they went to feed the ponies, Julian joked about Patrick.

'Poor Elizabeth. That's what comes of being a monitor. Bad luck!'

Elizabeth would normally have got the point at once and giggled. But today she looked at Julian in surprise.

'Bad luck? What do you mean exactly, Julian?'

'Having to partner Patrick down to the village shop,

of course,' he replied patiently. 'No wonder you looked cross when you got back for tea. Was he a pain as usual?'

'No, of course not. Patrick's not a pain!'

Julian looked at her in surprise.

'Oh, I know he is sometimes,' Elizabeth added hastily. She drew a deep breath. She must be careful. But she must also come to Patrick's defence. 'Your cousin's quite decent really. He's got hidden depths, you know.'

'Hidden depths?' Julian laughed out loud. 'So well hidden you'd never find them in a million years. Have you gone potty, Elizabeth? Or is this a bad attack of the goody-goody-monitor-itis disease?'

'Of course it isn't, Julian,' retorted Elizabeth indignantly.

'I think I prefer you when you're being the naughtiest girl,' he grinned.

Drat Patrick, thought Elizabeth, not letting her tell anybody about his brave deed! She was longing to tell Julian, but her lips had been sealed.

Patrick was pretending it was because he wanted nobody to find out that he'd been breaking a school rule. But Elizabeth was not convinced about that.

The real reason, she believed, was that, as with any true hero, Patrick was determined that his heroism should go unsung. And, although it made her cross, it also made her admire him all the more for it.

She decided she would try to express her admiration secretly. Somehow she'd find a way to be especially nice to him!

CHAPTER FOUR

AN UNEXPECTED DISCOVERY

WITH THE whole school assembled in the big hall Thomas and Emma announced the new award. They left it to the very end of Friday's Meeting. Every pupil listened attentively, from the junior children sitting cross-legged on the floor at the front, to the seniors on benches at the back. No boys and girls were allowed to miss the weekly 'parliament'. The joint headmistresses, with Mr Johns, the senior master, sat at the very back of the hall. They were there as observers. They never took part in the Meetings unless, for very difficult matters, their advice was needed.

Elizabeth and Joan sat in chairs on the platform with the other monitors, either side of the head boy and girl. Thomas and Emma sat at a special table, from where they conducted the Meeting.

There had been all the usual business to get through.

Money was collected from pupils who'd received some this week, then given out again to every member of the school in the form of the two shillings weekly allowance. At Whyteleafe School all money had to be fairly shared. Then special requests for extra money were listened to. They were discussed and then either granted or refused. There were no complaints or grumbles to be heard this week, but there were several sports announcements. Elizabeth was proud to hear her name read out as a member of the table-tennis team for tomorrow's match against Hickling Green.

Jake's name was again missing from the hockey team list. From her vantage point on the platform Elizabeth had watched him arrive for the Meeting. His limp, if anything, seemed more pronounced than ever. His ankle was still supported by a thick crepe bandage.

'We are all sorry that Jake will not be able to play for us at Hickling Green tomorrow,' announced Thomas, 'and we take this opportunity to wish him well and hope that his injury is better in time for our next hockey fixture, which will be against Milford Grange.'

Then Emma took over. 'Finally, we have some exciting news to tell you,' she said.

Elizabeth and Joan glanced at each other. At last! They had been waiting eagerly for the moment when the William and Rita Award would be announced. It had been a strain having to keep it secret since the MM. Now the whole school would hear about it. How would it be received? Had the monitors been correct when they'd all voted for it, so sure that their classmates would approve?

They need not have worried. The news was greeted with cheers and applause. It was very well received indeed! Soon a buzz of chatter ran up and down the rows.

A new honour, to be called the William and Rita Award!

To be given not for being brainy or good at games or anything like that, but for Outstanding Conduct, such as bravery or unselfishness ... or exceptional kindness. It would be handed out each half-term. What a fantastic idea!

'What are you so quiet for, Patrick?' asked their classmate, Arabella Buckley. 'Don't you like the idea?'

'Just thinking, that's all,' muttered Patrick. He had been listening attentively to the announcement. He appeared to be scowling.

'I think it's an excellent idea,' continued Arabella primly. She was already trying to work out how she might get to win the new honour. 'The brainy people get paid too much attention around here.'

'What do you think, Julian?' asked Arabella's friend,

Rosemary. 'I like the way it's called after William and Rita, don't you?'

'It's a good idea,' conceded Julian. 'And yes, it's a good name too. I'm sure they'd approve!'

Julian glanced up towards the platform, at Elizabeth's glowing face. So this was what the secret had been the other day. He was pleased to be privy to it at last. It was difficult, in some ways, the naughtiest girl being a monitor.

As the noise level in the hall grew, Thomas had to bring the Meeting to order. He banged the gavel sharply on the small table.

'Silence! We're pleased you all like the idea! But, if you've any questions or suggestions to make, please address them to the whole Meeting and not just to each other!'

Arabella was the first to put her hand up. She rose to her feet.

'Please, Thomas, Emma says we're allowed to put forward names for the award. But when should we do it exactly?'

'At any time, Arabella. At any time you see someone in your own form behaving in a way that deserves a nomination. The school office has a supply of special forms, called citation forms. You simply collect a form, fill in the person's name and your reason for naming them, then hand it to your monitor.'

'What happens to the forms then?' asked Arabella eagerly.

'Any monitor who has been given a citation form will read it out, at the next Monitors' Meeting. Each one will be heard in the privacy of that meeting. The best will go on a shortlist. Just before half-term, Emma and I will go through the shortlist with Miss Belle and Miss Best. They will help us to decide who has won the first William and Rita Award. But the award will be presented once every term. It will, we hope, become a regular feature of school life and something that all can strive for.'

'Thank you, Thomas,' nodded Arabella. She sat down, her dainty face a little pinker than usual.

There were a few more questions. After that the Meeting was declared closed.

Patrick waited for Elizabeth as she came out of the hall and pulled her to one side. He seemed agitated.

'I couldn't bear it, Elizabeth. You do understand, don't you? You do promise?'

'Of course I promise, Patrick.'

She patted his arm soothingly and smiled. She was feeling in a very good mood. How well the announcement had gone. The whole school approved of it! Thomas and Emma were absolutely right: courage and kindness and unselfishness were the most important qualities in the world. It was right that they should be recognised.

'You are much too modest, Patrick,' she said. 'But your secret is safe with me. I can't help wishing you would change your mind, though! You were so brave!'

At that moment Julian came out of the hall, looking for Elizabeth. He was confronted by the sight of her with Patrick. The pair of them were whispering together, smiling and looking at each other in a silly way.

'Come on, Elizabeth,' he said sharply. 'Let's go and have tea.'

'Just coming, Julian!'

As they made their way to the dining hall together, a feeling of exasperation swept over Julian.

'You seem to be getting very thick with my horrible cousin,' he commented.

'Oh, please don't be silly, Julian,' replied Elizabeth.

She was thinking hard. The glimmering of an idea was forming in her mind. She had thought of a way in which she could recognise Patrick's modesty and courage with a small noble deed of her own. It was no more than he deserved and it would be a gesture that she would find deeply satisfying.

Unfortunately, it was going to annoy Julian even more.

'Drat! I've got a horrid headache,' announced

Elizabeth the next day. 'I don't think I'm going to be well enough to play in my match today!'

Julian stared at his friend in surprise.

It was Saturday dinnertime. Elizabeth had been laughing and talking cheerfully during the meal and had eaten heartily. The boys and girls had been out blackberrying during the week. From the bags full of succulent fruit brought to the school kitchens Cook had concocted a whole shelf-full of summer puddings. They had been served today, with a choice of cream or custard. Elizabeth had eaten three helpings. Delicious!

'You must have eaten too much,' observed Julian.

'Oh, poor Elizabeth,' said Joan anxiously. 'But you mustn't miss the match! The coach leaves in twenty minutes . . . You'd better go and see Matron for some aspirin straight away!'

Further along the table, Patrick's ears had pricked up.

'It's no good, Joan!' Elizabeth ran her hand across her brow for dramatic effect. 'I just know I won't be able to play my best today. Patrick will have to play in my place. He's first reserve and he is very good, you know.'

For a moment Patrick had felt upset that Elizabeth was feeling unwell. But now, unable to help himself, a look of incredulous joy crossed his face. The naughtiest girl felt very pleased with herself as she noted his expression.

'Oh, Elizabeth, I'll be glad to take your place if you're not feeling up to it. Shall we go and see Emma right away and talk to her about it?'

'Yes, Patrick. Let's!'

They rushed off to see Emma, who was just leaving the seniors' table. It was almost time to go and get ready. As team captain, she agreed at once that Patrick should take Elizabeth's place. A jolting coach journey to Hickling Green School would make the headache much worse for Elizabeth, she reasoned.

As Patrick and Elizabeth walked back to their own table, Julian strained his ears to hear what was being said. Elizabeth was gazing at Patrick with that silly expression on her face again. Patrick was talking to her as though they were very dear friends.

'Oh, Elizabeth, I've been waiting for this chance for so long. I won't let you down, I promise. I'll play the best table tennis of my life.'

'I know you will, Patrick.'

'And I'll do it specially for you, Elizabeth! I'm going to win my match today, as a present for you.'

'Thank you, Patrick.'

'I don't think I've got time to finish my pudding. I'd better dash straight off and get changed and find my lucky table-tennis bat.'

He rushed away, brimming over with excitement.

AN UNEXPECTED DISCOVERY

Elizabeth slipped back into her seat between Julian and Joan, a satisfied little smile on her face.

'Poor Elizabeth,' repeated Joan, who was just getting up from the table. 'What a shame. Promise me you'll have a quiet lie-down this afternoon.'

'We'll want to go and wave the coach off first, won't we, Joan?' replied Elizabeth eagerly. 'We can wave to them and wish them good luck!'

Secretly, the naughtiest girl wanted to see Patrick's face again as he climbed on to the coach in his smart tracksuit. That happy look on his face made it all so worthwhile.

'I can't, Elizabeth,' Joan apologised. 'I've promised to go on an outing with Susan this afternoon. Look, she's waiting for me now.'

Sure enough, Joan's friend Susan, who had gone up into the third form this term, was signalling to her. Miss Thomas was taking a group to the indoor swimming pool in the town and Susan was a very keen swimmer. Thinking that Elizabeth would be away at her match, Joan had arranged to go too.

As she hurried off, Elizabeth turned to Julian.

He was bent over his pudding, a puzzled gleam in his green eyes. He was a very clever, bright boy. He was not easily tricked. He was convinced that Elizabeth was play-acting and did not have a headache at all.

39

She was trying to give Patrick a chance in the table-tennis team, that was all!

He was used to never knowing what went on inside her head. At other times it was one of the things he liked best about her! But not today. Why was Elizabeth being so nice to his worthless cousin? It didn't make sense. And Julian found it intensely irritating.

'You'll come with me to see Patrick off on the coach, won't you, Julian?' smiled Elizabeth. 'And it's a lovely afternoon. We could go out on the ponies after that. We could have a good long outing.'

'Certainly not,' said Julian. 'Why would I want to see Patrick off on the coach? As for going for a ride, I thought you had a headache.'

'Well, yes, but . . .' Elizabeth thought quickly. 'I'm sure the fresh air will do it good!'

'I'm sorry, Elizabeth. I've fixed up to go riding with Harry and Robert. As you're not well enough to play in your match, I suggest you go and have a good lie-down, as Joan suggested.'

'Yes, of course,' sighed Elizabeth.

Soon after that she left the dining hall and went outside into the school grounds for a walk. She wanted to collect her thoughts. Julian was annoyed with her! He couldn't understand why she was being so friendly towards Patrick. If only she could explain to him what a

40

fine person Patrick really was and that he *deserved* some reward. But she couldn't. She'd promised!

The coach was waiting on the back drive.

Shortly before it was due to leave, she went across there and hid in the shrubbery. She could see all the boys and girls climbing aboard, the hockey team as well. They were all laughing and talking together. Patrick was already in his seat, on the far side of the coach, so she couldn't see his expression after all. Unable to wave the coach off with her friends, she knew she would feel a bit silly doing it on her own. So she decided to watch it leave, from here, without being seen.

The warm glow that she'd felt a few minutes earlier had faded. As she watched the last passengers climb aboard and the coach doors shut, she felt very wistful. They were all off to Hickling Green without her. She was going to miss all the excitement! And what was she going to do with herself? The afternoon stretched ahead, bleak and empty . . .

As the coach moved away and trundled off down the drive, a figure standing behind it was suddenly revealed. He was waving, rather forlornly.

It was Jake, seeing the coach off. But, as soon as the vehicle disappeared, Jake's arm dropped to his side and he did an extraordinary thing.

Never dreaming that Elizabeth was watching him

from her hiding place, Jake shook his fist at the sky then ran furiously down the drive after the coach and took a flying kick at some loose gravel, to relieve his feelings. He then ran off down a side path and disappeared from view.

He was running! realised Elizabeth. *He didn't have a limp at all! He must have been pretending all this time. There's nothing wrong with his ankle whatsoever!*

It was a very surprising discovery.

CHAPTER FIVE

ELIZABETH GIVES JAKE AWAY

ELIZABETH FOLLOWED in Jake's tracks.

He's limping again, now that people can see him! she realised, as she reached the other end of the path where it emerged from the bushes. Here some junior boys and girls were playing on the back lawn.

Jake limped slowly past them, heading for the school buildings. For a moment she wondered if she could have just dreamt it. But only for a moment.

No. I definitely saw what I saw. So why is Jake play-acting like this? thought Elizabeth hot-temperedly. *It's so mean of him! How can he bear to let our form down in this way, as well as the hockey team and the whole of Whyteleafe School!*

She very nearly dashed after him there and then. But, even with her temper up, she did not quite dare to confront him. Besides, he was surrounded by some

43

junior boys now. Jake was one of their heroes.

What should she do?

Julian will know the best thing to do! Elizabeth decided. *I'll ask his advice. I'd better run all the way, if I want to catch him before he goes off!*

She raced across the grounds to the school stables. But the boys had just left.

'They went that way, Elizabeth,' Mr Tucker, the stableman told her, pointing up the bridle path.

'Thanks!' gasped Elizabeth.

She veered off through the trees. She could hear voices some distance ahead and the clip-clop of the ponies' hooves. Then, through a gap, she glimpsed them turning off at right angles, where the path divided. They were riding in single file, Robert, then Harry, Julian bringing up the rear. She scrambled over a bank and through tangled undergrowth, to cut off a corner. It brought her within hailing distance. She cupped her hands to her mouth.

'JULIAN!' she shouted, with all her might.

Startled, Julian reined in his pony. He wheeled the animal round and spotted Elizabeth frantically waving her arms. He told Harry and Robert to wait for him.

He trotted back to meet her. 'Whatever's wrong, Elizabeth?'

Gulping to get her breath back, she told Julian what

she had just discovered. She was bristling with indignation. He listened carefully.

Then, to her surprise, he gave a dry laugh.

'So that's two of you trying to get out of playing in school matches, is it?' he commented. 'You're a fine one to be cross, Elizabeth. How's the headache by the way?'

Elizabeth fell silent. Julian spoke more gently then.

'I think you must have imagined it about Jake, you know.'

'I did not, Julian. I certainly did not! I was hoping to hear your ideas – about the best thing to do.'

'Well, I know that *you* have a reason for getting out of *your* match, Elizabeth. Even if it is a totally potty one! So *Jake* may have a reason too. You will have to go and speak to him and ask him to explain. After all . . .'

Down the bridle path Harry and Robert were signalling impatiently. They were cross to have been held up like this. Julian wheeled his pony round. He was suddenly feeling rather cross himself.

'. . . *you* are the monitor, Elizabeth, not me. Good luck!'

Julian rode off then, without a backward glance. He was annoyed to have been reminded like this of Elizabeth making sacrifices on behalf of his worthless cousin, Patrick. Just when he had managed to put it out of his mind!

Elizabeth walked slowly back to school, feeling very subdued.

Her temper had evaporated now. Julian's words had rather shamed her. He had guessed that she had made it up about the headache. He had also guessed the reason why! She longed to explain to him about Patrick's brave deed, but she was not allowed to. And, of course, Julian was right. She was a fine one to feel indignant about Jake!

But she also knew that Julian's advice was correct. As Jake's monitor, she should go and speak to him and give him a chance to explain the reason for his strange behaviour. She should then persuade Jake to go and own up to the teachers. However, Elizabeth remembered the last time that she had spoken to the big boy as his monitor. How grumpy he had been with her – and with good reason, with so much to hide.

How much grumpier he would be if she dared to confront him now! And he would probably think that she had been spying on him. He would be furious!

All that afternoon Elizabeth tried to screw up courage to go and speak to the older boy. But her courage failed her. She decided that perhaps she would speak to Joan about it, at teatime. If Joan agreed, they would go and see Jake together this evening.

It was only when Joan did not turn up at teatime that

ELIZABETH GIVES JAKE AWAY

Elizabeth remembered that the swimming group had been excused tea today. They were having tea in town.

Julian turned up late, glowing from his ride, and did not even bother to ask Elizabeth if she had spoken to Jake yet. Elizabeth was relieved about that.

After that she did her piano practice and then decided to go and wait for the return of the school coach. She longed to know how the table-tennis team had got on at Hickling Green. What fun Patrick would have been having today, so much more fun than her. She'd never known such a dreary time. How she would have loved to play in the match!

The first person off the coach was Mr Warlow.

'Hello, Elizabeth. Feeling better? You'll be pleased to know that we won the table tennis. Patrick played very well.'

Elizabeth felt some relief at those words. She had done the school no harm then, by not playing in the match! But she had never seen the sports master look so careworn.

'Is there anything wrong, Mr Warlow?' she asked.

'I'm afraid the hockey match was a disaster. We were beaten six–nil. We had our chances to score, but we didn't take them. We needed our star shooter and that's a fact. It would have made such a difference if Jake had played. That wretched ankle of his. I have never known a simple sprain take so long to get better!'

The young sports master looked so unhappy, Elizabeth longed to cheer him up! She smiled impetuously and, before she could stop them, the words flew out of her mouth, unbidden.

'It's better now, Mr Warlow! It's just got better!'

'Elizabeth, is this true?' asked the teacher, looking excited. 'Have you spoken to Jake then?'

Elizabeth gulped. What had she said? What had she *done*? There was no going back now.

'I – I haven't actually spoken to him. But I saw him outside and the ankle's suddenly looking . . . well, really fine. I'm sure it's going to be all right for the match against Milford Grange, Mr Warlow! I'm sure if you get Jake to have a check-up . . .'

'I'll drive him to the doctor myself!' exclaimed Mr Warlow in delight. 'I'll go and find him straight away! If we hurry, we'll just make surgery before it closes.'

He strode briskly away.

'This is very good news, Elizabeth!' he called back over his shoulder. 'Thank you so much for telling me! What a good monitor you are!'

'Hello, Elizabeth! What's this about good news? I've got some good news myself!'

Patrick had appeared at her side. Some members of the Whyteleafe first hockey team were beginning to trudge past, heads bowed, eyes downcast. But Patrick was beaming with pride.

'I won both my games, Elizabeth!' he was saying. 'I told you I would, didn't I?'

Elizabeth was watching Mr Warlow, as he disappeared into the school building. He was determined to find Jake at once. He wanted to take him to the doctor's! What a shock the big boy was going to get. Elizabeth could not help feeling a little trembly. She had let her tongue run away with her.

With an effort she turned her attention to Patrick.

'Congratulations!' she said, looking pale. 'I'm so pleased for you. Was it a good outing then?'

'A marvellous outing! We had the most splendid tea!' Patrick was looking elated. 'But you haven't heard the half of it, Elizabeth! Donald didn't play at all well today. If it hadn't been for me, we'd have lost. My last game decided it. From something Emma said to me I think I'm going to be chosen instead of Donald next time.'

They started to walk over to the school together.

'Oh, Patrick, I'm so glad I gave you your chance!' Elizabeth blurted out. 'It's no more than you deserve.'

'Gave me my chance?' asked Patrick, looking puzzled.

Elizabeth took a deep breath. She had been stung by Julian's words earlier. It would make her feel better if Patrick, at least, knew the truth . . .

49

'I didn't really have a headache,' she confessed. 'I was just desperate to make sure that you got some reward at least for your brave deed.'

'Elizabeth!' exclaimed Patrick. He looked horrified. 'You shouldn't have done that.'

'I had to,' she replied. 'You are such a fine person, Patrick. I don't know how I'm going to hold my tongue at the next MM, I really don't . . . You do deserve the William and Rita Award, you really do!'

'No!' The boy paled. 'You promised!'

'It's all right, it's all right,' she said soothingly. Seeing how upset he was, she slipped her arm through his as they walked towards the school steps together. 'Only joking, Patrick! I am sure a lot of fine deeds will be coming up at the MMs. I expect Thomas and Emma will have far too many to choose from when the time comes! I must say I'm looking forward to hearing some of them.'

Patrick nodded, visibly relieved. He liked having Elizabeth on his arm like this. Somebody was coming down the steps, and would be passing right by them in a moment . . .

'Hello, Julian!' he said cheerfully. 'I won my games today! Nice evening, isn't it?'

'Is it?' asked Julian curtly. 'Joan's back, Elizabeth. She was looking for you.' And he passed on his way.

Elizabeth took her leave of Patrick almost immediately.

She found Joan resting on the bed upstairs.

'Oh, Elizabeth, I have had such a wonderful time! But I am quite exhausted now!'

Gentle Joan had never shone at sports. But today she had made an exciting discovery. It seemed that Miss Thomas believed that she had the talents of a born swimmer. The teacher was hoping to get up a Whyteleafe swimming team some time. She had told Joan that, with the right training, she could well be a member of it.

'Miss Thomas is going to give Susan and me and some others regular fitness training in the gym,' Joan explained. 'Oh, Elizabeth, I never thought I'd ever be good at sports, but I really think I might enjoy swimming.'

'Joan, this is the most thrilling news!' exclaimed Elizabeth, pleased to see her friend so happy.

For once Joan was too full of her own news to question her friend about the headache, or how she'd spent the afternoon. That came as a relief to Elizabeth.

She was beginning to feel very ashamed that, instead of having the courage to go and speak to Jake, she had ended up blurting out his secret to a teacher. She could not bring herself to confess what she had done, even to her best friend.

But what would happen now?

CHAPTER SIX

A HORRID MESSAGE APPEARS

ON SUNDAY morning Jake was seen running up and down the hockey pitch with Mr Warlow, practising his stick work. The teacher wanted to see his star player back on top form as quickly as possible. He would be needed for the Milford Grange match, needed very badly!

Several second-form boys turned out to watch him. Martin, Kenneth, Harry and John McTavish were all fans of his. He was such a marvellous player for a boy of his age; Kenneth was already a friend of his in the second form. The others had admired him even when they were only in the first form.

It was great news, the boys all agreed, that the sprained ankle had now made a complete recovery. Mr Warlow had got the doctor to check it over last night. There had been no sign of bruising or swelling there. Jake was pronounced fit to play hockey again.

'What a shame it wasn't in time to play against Hickling Green yesterday!' observed Harry.

'But he'll be able to play against Milford Grange!' smiled Martin. 'It's a home match so we'll all be able to watch!'

'We'll thrash them!' said John jubilantly. 'Jake will see to that.'

They were all very pleased.

'Did you speak to Jake then, Elizabeth?' asked Julian, with interest, at one point during the day.

'Not exactly,' she mumbled in embarrassment, and hurried off.

For the only person who was not pleased was Jake.

Secretly, he was very upset. He did not want to play hockey against Milford Grange. He did not want to play hockey at all. When he passed Elizabeth in the dining hall at breakfast time, he had given her such a fierce look. Mr Warlow might think that Elizabeth was a good monitor, to have spotted that Jake's ankle had suddenly made a recovery, but Jake did not share that opinion! He was very taken aback by it all and became convinced that Elizabeth must have been spying on him in secret. How long had she been doing so? he wondered.

She had also got him into trouble. For the doctor had informed Mr Warlow that from all appearances any injury to the ankle must have repaired itself some time ago. The teacher was baffled that Jake had made out the injury to be far worse than it really was. He had accused him of laziness and of letting down the school.

Jake was such a big, silent, powerful character. The fierce look he had given Elizabeth had made her flinch! She spent the rest of the day avoiding him. She was very puzzled by his strange behaviour. At the same time she was truly ashamed that his secret had come out in the way that it had. She wanted to find some way of showing him that she was sorry.

By the evening, when she felt hopeful that Jake would have cooled down somewhat, she took her chance. He was standing, drinking cocoa in the second-form common room, surrounded by the gang of boys who admired him.

'Have my chocolate biscuit, Jake,' she said, walking up to him. 'It will build you up for the match against Milford Grange! May I come and cheer you on, please?'

'Don't bother,' replied Jake curtly, ignoring the plate. 'I can manage without you.'

Elizabeth had a hot temper. It immediately flared up.

'How rude!' she gasped, gazing up at the boy as he towered above her. 'You're not to talk to a monitor like that!'

That immediately inflamed Jake.

A HORRID MESSAGE APPEARS

'I'm tired of girl monitors,' he stated. 'Girl monitors would do a lot better to mind their own business.'

'Hear, hear!' agreed Martin. He had no idea what Jake was talking about but he could see that the big boy was very angry.

Elizabeth's own anger easily matched Jake's.

She wanted to blurt out that it was not just her business but everybody else's if a person pretended they had something wrong with them when they hadn't and deliberately let a school team down! But then, to her horror, she remembered that she'd just done the same thing herself. Even if, by good fortune, Patrick had won his games and prevented the table-tennis team from being defeated.

She bit back her words, turned on her heel and marched out of the common room. She slammed the door loudly behind her.

'What's up between you and her, Jake?' asked his friend Kenneth.

'She told tales, that's all,' replied Jake, looking morose. 'She exceeded her authority. She shouldn't poke her nose in my private business. I'm fed up with bossy girl monitors thinking they know what's best for us boys.'

'Joan doesn't do that,' Harry pointed out fairly.

'No,' agreed Martin. 'And she's been one for ages.

Elizabeth's new, which makes it worse.'

'I expect it's gone right to her curly head,' sighed Jake wearily.

He clammed up then. He became his usual strong, silent self and refused to answer any more questions. But after he'd left the common room the other boys were all agog.

They liked the naughtiest girl. But they all knew how she'd got her nickname! And there was no doubt that she could still be headstrong and impulsive and do crazy things sometimes. They admired Jake and they trusted him. If he was angry with Elizabeth, then she must have seriously overstepped the mark in some way.

'She wanted to wear a monitor's armband, didn't she, Harry?' remembered Martin. 'And Julian teased her and said it would make her look like a member of the secret police!'

'And it sounds as though she's been behaving like one!' commented John McTavish. 'What a nerve, telling tales on someone like Jake. Thinking she knows what's best for him.'

'I wonder what it was all about?' pondered Harry.

The news of the quarrel spread around the boys' dormitories that night, and grew in the telling. The joke about the armband, and the secret police, was also passed around.

Julian felt rather badly when he heard his joke being repeated. He was going to say something in Elizabeth's defence, but then Patrick stepped in.

'Elizabeth is a very good sort!' he declared. 'Shut up, all of you.'

So Julian shrugged his shoulders and said nothing.

Elizabeth slept badly that night. There were tears of frustration in her eyes. She so much wanted to be a successful monitor, but things were starting to go wrong.

At breakfast time, on Monday morning, she could tell that some of the boys had started to turn against her.

'Where's your armband, Elizabeth?' Martin teased her. 'We won't know to do what we're told if you don't wear an armband.'

Arabella tittered loudly.

'It's not that funny, Arabella,' said Julian airily. 'It's rather an old joke by now. Can't you think of a new one, Martin?'

Elizabeth was glad to escape from the dining hall.

She went up to Room Fourteen to clean her shoes and brush her hair and get ready for lessons. Joan, Kathleen and Jenny, who had all been sitting at the other table today, drifted in. Elizabeth enjoyed chatting about other things with her roommates and began to feel a bit better.

Drat boys! she thought. It was fun just being with

girls sometimes! She began to look forward to her first lesson, which was French, with Mam'zelle.

'Let's get down to the form room nice and early,' suggested Joan.

'Yes!' nodded Elizabeth. 'My desk needs a bit of a tidy-up.'

The form room was empty when they arrived. The two friends had adjoining desks. Elizabeth boisterously flung up her desk lid.

'Oh!' She quickly closed it again, her cheeks pale.

'What was that?' asked Joan quickly. 'What was that piece of paper taped to the inside of your desk lid?'

'It – it seems to be some kind of horrid message,' said Elizabeth.

Gently, Joan opened the desk lid again. Together, the two friends gazed in silence at the anonymous message, carefully written in block capitals.

WHY HAS THE SECOND FORM GOT TWO GIRL MONITORS? NOT FAIR! GIVE DANIEL HIS CHANCE BACK, ELIZABETH. GIVE THE BOYS A MONITOR OF THEIR OWN!

At that moment Mr Leslie, their form master, came into the classroom to put some things away. Joan

A HORRID MESSAGE APPEARS

carefully removed the message, folded it and placed it in her pocket. They would have to discuss it later.

CHAPTER SEVEN

THINGS GO FROM BAD TO WORSE

'WHAT'S ALL this about, Elizabeth?' asked Joan, at morning break. 'Have you any idea who could have written it?'

'I believe I know exactly who has written it!' replied Elizabeth.

The two friends were sitting on the school steps in the pale October sunshine. Joan had taken the piece of paper from her pocket and unfolded it. Why had somebody turned against Elizabeth? It was all very upsetting.

'Who?' asked Joan in surprise.

'Jake, of course!' Elizabeth blurted out. 'How mean of him not to sign it. What an underhand thing to do!'

'*Jake?*' asked Joan. She liked the gentle giant of a boy and felt she knew him quite well. He had joined the second form even earlier than she had. 'Whyever should

Jake be feeling cross with you, Elizabeth? Especially as I'm sure he must be in a very good mood at the moment with his poor ankle better.'

'That's just it, Joan! He's not in a good mood at all about his ankle! He should be, but he isn't. And he's simply furious with me!'

Joan's eyes widened. She spoke gently.

'What's been going on, Elizabeth? What have you been keeping from me?'

Shamefaced, Elizabeth told Joan everything that had happened concerning Jake the previous day. It was a relief to do so at last.

But Joan, as Elizabeth feared she would be, was very disapproving.

'It was very wrong of you to speak to Mr Warlow before you had spoken to Jake himself, Elizabeth!' she scolded. 'You know that's not the way we do things at Whyteleafe. Jake must have had some very private reason of his own for wanting to get out of hockey, something that he was determined to keep secret. As his monitor, you should have asked him to talk it through with you and then tried to persuade him to go and own up to Mr Warlow. No wonder he is cross with you!'

'I was too scared to,' Elizabeth confessed. 'I was sure Jake didn't respect me as a monitor and the note proves I was right. He thinks the other monitor should be a boy! And, because I've upset Jake, some more of the boys are turning against me! What should I do, Joan? Do you think I should resign?'

'Of course not, Elizabeth!' her friend replied firmly. She folded the note up and replaced it in her pocket. 'You can't give in to this sort of thing. It's not always easy being a monitor and we all make mistakes. Just try to tread carefully for a while, Elizabeth. Everybody likes you very much and wanted you to be a monitor this term. I'm sure this will all blow over in a few days.'

'Oh, do you really think so, Joan?'

Elizabeth felt very cheered. But her cheerfulness did not last long.

Far from blowing over, the trouble with the boys got worse.

Elizabeth was still being teased. And the feeling that it was unfair not to have a boy monitor seemed to be spreading. Jake continued to be unfriendly towards her and Elizabeth strongly suspected that, as well as writing the note, he was encouraging the other boys in some kind of campaign to get rid of her. Had she made a powerful enemy?

In Martin's dormitory they were starting to have pillow fights at night. These were forbidden, of course, but apparently great fun!

Martin openly bragged that, as girls were not allowed

to enter the boys' quarters, they could do what they liked as they only had girl monitors in the second form. No monitors could come and stop their fun!

Julian gave Elizabeth a friendly word of warning.

'I shouldn't report them, if I were you, Elizabeth,' he said. 'Not if you know what's good for you!'

Elizabeth had never actually admitted to Julian that she'd given Jake's secret away because she and Julian were far less close than usual. She was sad, but there was nothing she could do about it, without explaining to him the story of Patrick's bravery. However, on the Jake front, Julian had very quickly worked things out for himself. Like Elizabeth, he was mystified as to why the big boy had pretended about the injury in the first place.

'Don't worry, Julian,' she sighed. 'I know I'm in enough trouble already. I haven't the slightest intention of reporting them.'

She would love to have had a proper chat with him about everything. But he was already strolling away, whistling.

Patrick was a real nuisance! she thought.

She thought so again, the following day.

The next Monitors' Meeting was due. In Elizabeth's class only one written nomination had been handed in. Quivering with importance, Rosemary had handed the special form over to Joan. But Joan was not able to attend this week's MM. Miss Thomas had arranged the first fitness session for the would-be swimming team. It would clash directly with the MM, but it was the teacher's only free time. Joan dared not miss her very first workout.

'I'm afraid that you are going to have to read this out at the MM, Elizabeth,' she said later, with a wry smile, passing across Rosemary's form. 'What a lovely job for you!'

'Oh, no!' groaned Elizabeth, reading what was written there. 'This is going to be so embarrassing. Must I really? Ugh!'

They both laughed.

Nevertheless, after lessons that day, Elizabeth set off eagerly for the MM. This was going to be very interesting. What kind of citations would the other monitors be reading out from their classmates? Surely they'd be more exciting than Rosemary's? She certainly hoped so!

She arrived on time this week and collected her mug of tea. There were chocolate digestive biscuits again. Good!

'It's all right, Elizabeth, there are plenty. You may take two!' smiled Emma.

She settled down on the floor, next to Peter, letting

Donald have the place on the bench. It was quite comfortable on the floor this week as Thomas had managed to find some cushions.

'Hello, Peter,' she said to the young first-form monitor. 'Have you been given any citations yet for the William and Rita Award?'

Peter shook his head. He seemed to have something else on his mind.

'Not yet, Elizabeth. I keep asking for them, though.'

Soon all the monitors had crammed into the cosy study. Elizabeth was disappointed to see that not many had brought citations with them. She gave Joan's apologies. Then various minor school matters were discussed. Peter put his hand up.

'Please, Thomas and Emma, can you all give me some advice? Some of the boys in my class were squirting water pistols indoors. They wouldn't stop when I asked, so I confiscated them. When d'you think I should give them back?'

They all discussed Peter's problem.

'There we are then! We're all agreed,' Thomas concluded. 'You can keep them for a week. A week seems quite a long time when you're in the first form! Then, as long as they promise only to play with them out-of-doors in future, you can hand them back!'

At last it was time for the citations to be read out.

'You first, Elizabeth,' said Emma. 'I can see you've got one in your hand.'

'It's only just the one so far, I'm afraid,' apologised Elizabeth. 'It's been submitted by Rosemary Wing.'

She tried her best to hide her embarrassment as she read out loud the second form's only citation.

'Yesterday my hamster looked very droopy and I was worried about him. Then Arabella Buckley performed a very unselfish act. Arabella is very fond of chocolate herself, but she sacrificed all the chocolate she had left for the whole week and fed it to Hammy, so as to cheer him up. I would therefore like to nominate Arabella Buckley for the William and Rita Award.'

Some of the monitors snorted and sniggered.

'I expect poor Hammy was sick on the spot!' whispered Donald.

Elizabeth's cheeks burnt. She felt so ashamed of her classmates. It was obvious that Arabella had put Rosemary up to this! Surely, between them, they could at least have invented something better? She'd tried her best to read it nicely and put the correct expression in her voice. But it had still sounded completely silly.

THINGS GO FROM BAD TO WORSE

'Thank you, Elizabeth,' said Emma sympathetically. 'That was very nicely read.'

'And those of you who are giggling, I'm ashamed of you,' added Thomas. 'All citations are to be listened to in silence, please. I think we are all agreed that this one's not suitable for the shortlist, so let us pass on.'

Elizabeth at once felt better. Now that the second-form citation had been dealt with, she could settle down and look forward to hearing the other forms' contributions.

But there were, indeed, only a few. And, although they were all much more genuine than Rosemary's effort, they were not very inspiring.

After hearing out the last one, read by Eric, the head boy and girl shook their heads.

'I don't think anything we have heard today is quite suitable for the shortlist, do you?' asked Emma ruefully. 'The William and Rita Award must be given for an act of real courage or unselfishness, not everyday acts of kindness, pleasing though it is to hear about them.'

'We seem to have got off to a slow start, I'm afraid,' agreed Thomas. 'Luckily there's plenty of time yet. We must look forward to something really splendid coming in over the next couple of weeks.'

But Elizabeth could tell that they were both very disappointed.

It was so frustrating! How she longed to tell them that a member of the second form had performed an act of real courage.

As she left the MM, she decided that she must go and find Patrick at once. He had just finished a game of table tennis with Daniel.

'Listen, Patrick, I've been thinking,' she said, as she took him outside. There was a pleading note in her voice. 'You know, about your brave deed. I know you don't want it talked about and I know you must be worried that you broke a school rule that day, being down in the village on your own. But supposing, when I go to the next MM, I just talk about this certain boy, without giving his name away? Supposing I just talk about this certain boy being worried about breaking this strict rule and see if they think that matters . . . ? And then . . .'

'Elizabeth! Stop being so tiresome!' exclaimed Patrick impatiently. 'I am not in the least bit worried about being punished for breaking a school rule. That has nothing to do with it really!'

'But . . .'

'I just don't want to be held up as some kind of hero, Elizabeth!' He stared at her, looking baffled and angry. 'Why are you bringing all this up again?'

'I'm sorry, Patrick. I just wondered if perhaps –

well, all us monitors want the first William and Rita Award to be something really special! Can't you see that? And I thought, if it was just the school rule you were worried about . . .'

'Well, it's not!' Patrick almost shouted the words. 'Please forget the whole thing. You promised.'

'I – I'll try.'

'Drop it, Elizabeth! Please don't mention this again!'

Elizabeth walked away after that. She was still filled with admiration for Patrick. How could she not be? But it was very annoying of him all the same. The William and Rita Award was such a lovely idea. But supposing nobody came forward with anything worthwhile by half-term? Thomas and Emma would not be able to give the award after all. What a bad start that would be.

Nothing seemed to be going right at the moment. In fact, things went from bad to worse.

When she went along to collect some homework from her desk, after tea, there was another anonymous message stuck inside the lid. Once again it was written in block capitals:

SOME OF US ARE FED UP. THERE ARE PILLOW FIGHTS NOW – KEEPING US AWAKE AT NIGHT. THE SECOND FORM NEEDS A BOY MONITOR TO KEEP

ORDER. WHY NOT RESIGN, PLEASE, ELIZABETH?

Paling slightly, she hurried outside to find Joan.

CHAPTER EIGHT

THE NAUGHTIEST GIRL VERSUS THE BOYS

'MY SO-CALLED secret enemy has struck again, Joan!' she said crossly, showing Joan the message. 'Not all that secret in fact. I'm quite convinced that it's Jake who's writing these notes. I know I'm a coward, Joan, but shall we go and see him together and tell him to stop it? He might take some notice of you.'

'We can't do that, Elizabeth,' replied Joan, biting her lip as she read the note carefully. 'We can't be sure it's Jake. Is this really Jake's sort of thing? And we certainly can't walk up to him and accuse him without any proof!'

'I suppose not,' sighed Elizabeth. She read the note through carefully, once again. 'To be fair, it must be very annoying for Jake if these pillow fights are keeping him awake.'

'If it is Jake,' Joan reminded her gently.

'Well, Jake or whoever it is. Anybody who doesn't specially enjoy pillow fights,' said Elizabeth. She was looking thoughtful. 'As I *am* a monitor, I should be thinking what to do.'

'I shouldn't worry, Elizabeth!' said Joan hastily, noting the light in her eye. 'We can't take any notice of anonymous messages. If anyone comes forward with a proper complaint about losing a lot of sleep, then that would be serious and you'd have to report it to the teachers.'

'What, tell tales?' asked Elizabeth, aghast, remembering Julian's advice to her. 'But that would make my position even worse, Joan.'

'This would be quite different, Elizabeth. You couldn't possibly deal with a whole crowd of boys on your own. But, of course, someone would have to make a formal complaint first, not just write a silly note like this. And I don't suppose anybody will.'

Elizabeth did not follow Joan's logic. In any case she was hardly listening.

She'd suddenly remembered young Peter's water pistols and an excited gleam came into her eye. She knew exactly how to handle this problem! She certainly didn't want anybody making a formal complaint to either Joan or herself and then having to go to the teachers. She didn't agree with Joan at all about that.

The boys would never forgive them.

She must act quickly, before there was any danger of it happening.

Later, a cheerful sparkle in her eye, Elizabeth slipped off to talk to some of the other girls. They were good sports, all of them. Then she went to find Peter.

I'm not going to involve Joan in this, she thought. *But I'll jolly well show those boys who's the monitor around here!*

Even as Elizabeth was borrowing the water pistols from Peter, an even younger boy was seeking out Joan, for the junior class did not have a monitor of its own. The small boy was in pyjamas and dressing gown but was not looking forward to going to bed. For two nights running he'd been woken up by bumpings and crashings in the second-form dormitory and had been unable to get to sleep again. His bed was right against the dividing wall. There were dark rings under his eyes.

'Go straight to bed now, Rupert,' Joan told him, after hearing him out. 'I'll see this is sorted out. I'll see to it myself, I promise.'

And I won't involve Elizabeth, she thought. *It's true what she says. She is in enough trouble already.*

After that, Joan decided, she would go to bed herself. The fitness training in the gym had been very enjoyable, but had left her tired out and aching in every muscle.

'Sh, Kathleen! Sh, Jenny!' whispered Elizabeth. 'We mustn't wake Joan!'

'No danger of that, Elizabeth. She's dead to the world!' Kathleen whispered back.

'Miss Thomas really puts them through it, I gather!' commented Jenny.

'Such luck!' giggled Kathleen.

'Sh!' repeated Elizabeth.

It was after lights out, and the three girls had slipped out of bed and were putting on their dressing gowns and slippers. They had waited until they were sure that Joan was in a very deep sleep. On no account, Elizabeth explained, did she want to involve Joan in her plan.

'I shall take full responsibility for this,' she had told her roommates earlier. 'I don't want to have to report those boys to the teachers and I don't want Joan to either. They think it's so clever having pillow fights, but we'll soon cool them down!'

Belinda and Tessa were waiting for them in the corridor.

'Got the water pistols, Elizabeth?' whispered Belinda eagerly.

'I've hidden them in the bathroom!' the naughtiest girl whispered back.

The five girls tiptoed along the corridor to the big bathroom. They were all trying hard not to giggle.

This was going to be such an adventure! Elizabeth took the five water pistols out from their hiding place in the big linen box. She handed her friends one each.

'Right,' she said. 'Now let's load them. As full as full can be.'

With Elizabeth their commander-in-chief leading the way the girls crept along the dimly lit corridors until they reached the boys' quarters. Their pistols were at the ready, loaded with water up to the hilt.

'Martin's dormitory,' she whispered crisply. 'Number Seventeen. Just at the bottom of these stairs. Come on now. Party – advance!'

'I think I can hear them now,' whispered Kathleen excitedly, as they crept down the short flight of stairs. 'Voices!'

The door was ajar. There seemed to be torches flashing around inside. It was after lights out, but there were figures moving about and some whispering going on. The nightly pillow fight must be just about to commence!

Eyes sparkling with anticipation, Elizabeth waved her water pistol above her head in a signal to the other four.

'Ready, steady – *charge!*' she hissed.

With their monitor at their head the girls hurled themselves down the last few stairs and burst into Room Seventeen.

'FIRE!' cried Elizabeth and they squeezed the triggers, spraying fine jets of water at the figures that moved in the dark.

'Break it up, boys!'

'Cool down!'

'Pillow fights not allowed!'

As they shouted their war cries, the girls were laughing with glee.

'Bull's-eye!' cried Elizabeth, as she squirted her best jet of water towards the back of somebody's neck.

'Got you!' she added triumphantly. 'Now perhaps *that* will cool you down just a little bit . . .'

At that very moment the figure turned, receiving it full in the face.

'ELIZABETH ALLEN!' roared the person, shining his torch on her. 'What on earth do you think you are doing?'

Elizabeth and her friends recoiled in dismay. It was a man's voice. They knew it well. Elizabeth shone her own torch, while behind her somebody switched on a light.

Elizabeth found herself face to face with Mr Leslie, their form master. He had three senior boys with him, including Thomas, the head boy. These were the only figures who'd been moving around! They were holding torches. All of them had water dripping down their shirts. Martin and the others, from all appearances, were asleep in bed. Only now were tousled heads raising themselves from various pillows.

'Hey!'

'What's going on?'

'Who's put that light on?'

came the innocent-sounding cries.

Elizabeth stared at her teacher in horror. 'I'm t-t-terribly sorry, sir,' she stammered.

Mr Leslie looked very cross.

'And so you should be, Elizabeth. We were told there might be some horseplay tonight, but we expected to find *boys* misbehaving not girls. Please return to your own quarters this instant, all of you.'

The five girls dived out of the door in relief. They couldn't wait to escape! From the stairs they heard Thomas's voice.

'It's all right, boys. Sorry you've been disturbed. You can go back to sleep now.'

The girls returned to their quarters in silence. What a disaster, thought Jenny and the others. Somehow the boys had got wind of Elizabeth's plan and neatly turned the tables. When the girl monitor and her troops had turned up to put a stop to the boys' pillow fights, they'd run straight into their teacher and his inspection party, with the second-form boys pretending to be fast asleep!

The boys had won. The girls were going to get into trouble and Elizabeth, as ringleader, would get into the biggest trouble of all!

But all Elizabeth could think about, as she tried to get back to sleep that night, was her enemy. *Somebody* had reported her plan to Mr Leslie. And she was sure she knew who. What a mean thing to do!

But the next morning she got a shock.

'Of course it wasn't Jake!' exclaimed Joan in horror, as she listened to Elizabeth's tale of woe. 'Oh, Elizabeth, what a dreadful mix-up. What a dreadful thing to happen! It was me!'

'You, Joan?' squealed Elizabeth in surprise.

Her loud squeal brought Jenny and Kathleen running over.

In distress Joan explained to her roommates about little Rupert.

'The child was desperate about it. He turned to me for help, as a monitor. It left me with no choice but to go and report to Mr Leslie that Room Seventeen was being noisy at nights, though I didn't say anything about the pillow fights. I'm sorry I didn't tell you, Elizabeth. I didn't want to involve you.'

'I'm sorry I didn't tell you about *my* plan,' said Elizabeth, very shamefaced. 'Oh, what a muddle!'

'Thank goodness it wasn't one of the boys anyway,'

said Kathleen, with a sigh of relief.

'Yes, that makes us feel a bit better about it,' agreed Elizabeth. She frowned. 'But Joan, how did Martin and the others know to be well behaved last night? That's what I can't understand.'

Joan thought about it carefully. 'John McTavish walked past last night, when Rupert was talking to me in the corridor. I didn't think he had heard anything. But obviously he must have done.'

'Ah!' said Elizabeth.

So that too was explained.

When Mr Leslie came into class to take the register that morning, the boys owned up about the pillow fights. That, at least, came as a great relief to Elizabeth, Joan and the others. They were a nice crowd really.

'Humph, yes, well, I'm not stupid, Martin,' said Mr Leslie. 'I did realise that something must have been going on. That the fault would not be all on one side. As your high jinks have been depriving some of the other boys of their sleep, Thomas is going to raise the matter at this week's Meeting.'

'Is he going to raise the matter of Elizabeth as well?' asked Jake, with interest. 'Our *monitor*.'

Some of the boys laughed. Elizabeth flushed deeply at Jake's intervention.

'I understand that Elizabeth will be dealt with at the

next Monitors' Meeting,' replied Mr Leslie curtly.
'Now, will everybody please get their pencils and paper
ready. Miss Ranger will be here very shortly and today's
the day you have your spelling tests.'

After that Julian made some sympathetic 'hen
clucking' noises to try to cheer Elizabeth up. He had
heard all about the episode in Room Seventeen and had
found it highly diverting. Would the naughtiest girl
even last till half-term as a monitor? he wondered.

But Elizabeth was not amused. She concentrated
hard on the weekly spelling test. After that, for the rest
of the English lesson, she kept her head bent over her
work. She felt a sense of despair. She had so much
wanted to be a successful and popular monitor this term,
one who enjoyed the respect of the whole form, like
Joan. But she could see that Jake was not going to allow
that to happen.

Of course, the water pistols had not been such a good
idea. She had been silly and hot-headed and she could
not blame Jake for that. But it was getting those horrid
notes that had stirred her up and made her behave
foolishly. Now some of the boys were laughing at her.

She smouldered as she thought of the notes and she
came to a decision.

'I have decided to tackle Jake about those mean
notes,' she whispered to Joan, towards the end of the

lesson. 'I know you don't want to, so I've decided to speak to him on my own. I shall tell him what I think of him!'

Joan just looked helpless and shook her head.

At that moment Miss Ranger called the two monitors out.

'Elizabeth and Joan, would you please give everybody their spellings back? I have marked them now.'

As the two friends shared out the bundle between them, the English teacher spoke pleasantly to the class.

'Elizabeth and Joan will bring your spellings round. Julian has come top today with twenty out of twenty. Jake, you would have had full marks, but once again you forgot your silent g's. You always forget them! You spelt both *sign* and *resign* without the *g*! When you think of *sign*, think of *signature* and that will help you remember. And when you spell *resign*, think of *resignation*. It's a shame you have such a blank spot about this, or you would have come equal top . . .'

'Yes, Miss Ranger.'

As the English teacher chatted on, Elizabeth was staring at Jake's spellings which were on top of the batch in her hand. Twenty words were written down. Eighteen had red ticks by them and two had been marked with a red cross.

'. . . I'm afraid, Jake,' the teacher was saying, with a

humorous smile, 'that *sign* and *resign* become two completely different words when you leave the *g*'s out. *resin* is something produced from sap. And *sin* is something you commit when you forget your silent *g*'s!'

Everyone laughed. But Elizabeth's scalp prickled as she gazed at Jake's spellings – at that word *resin*, with its cross beside it. Briefly, she shut her eyes, then opened them again.

And I've made a mistake, too, she realised. *Jake didn't write those notes. He couldn't have done.*

For on yesterday's message she was quite sure the word *resign* had been spelt correctly.

CHAPTER NINE

ELIZABETH LEARNS JAKE'S SECRET

'HOW CLEVER of you to remember, Elizabeth,' said Joan when they discussed it together at dinner time. 'I'd never have thought of it. Thank goodness you remembered the wording of this message and worked out that it couldn't be Jake. Only just in time. You were planning to rush off and accuse him!'

'You're the really wise one, Joan,' said Elizabeth humbly. 'You warned me I was being hot-headed! I was too stubborn to listen.'

They were both staring at the second anonymous message, which she had collected from upstairs. WHY NOT RESIGN, PLEASE, ELIZABETH? it ended and it was all spelt correctly. The message was written *before* today's spelling test. If Jake had looked up the spelling to write the message, he would hardly have forgotten it for an important test.

'Jake's always struggled with English,' mused Joan. 'That's why he's still in the second form. I couldn't quite imagine him putting pen to paper to write messages. Jake's style is just to say things straight out!'

'Yes,' nodded Elizabeth. She looked rueful. 'And he's certainly done that as far as I'm concerned. But it was wrong of me to leap to conclusions.'

It was a warm day. The girls were sitting beneath the weeping ash tree, in the school grounds. All the leaves had changed colour in the past week. They were starting to float down now, carpeting the grass around them. Elizabeth caught a fluttering leaf in her hands and examined it. She was thinking hard. She so loved it here at Whyteleafe School, but it was horrid having an enemy. Who *did* write those messages?

'If Jake isn't the enemy, then I want to know who is, Joan!' she said angrily.

The two girls discussed the mystery all dinner hour. They badly wanted to solve it. They went through possible suspects, as real detectives would.

'We can be sure it's a boy, and we can be sure he's in the second form,' said Joan softly. 'So that narrows it down.'

'Not very much, though,' replied Elizabeth ruefully. 'The first thing is to think of the motive. It's got to be somebody who hates the idea of there being two girl monitors, who thinks it's unfair. Somebody other than Jake.'

'What about Daniel?' suggested Joan tentatively.

'Oh, surely not Daniel!' exclaimed Elizabeth in dismay. He was a gentle, sensitive boy. 'I like Daniel! And I'm sure he likes me! Except . . .'

She broke off, remembering the wistful expression on Daniel's face last week, when she'd come from an MM. *They do sound fun*, he'd said. Under his gentle exterior, could Daniel secretly be regretting that he'd stood down after his few days as a monitor, to give Elizabeth her place back?

'I don't want to think it's Daniel, Joan!' she stated. 'Let's think of somebody else. In books it's always the last person you suspect . . .' she laughed. 'Say Julian, for instance . . .'

Even as Elizabeth spoke her friend's name out loud, her laughter faded on her lips and her heart gave a jolt.

'Julian!' she whispered. 'Is it possible? He has been quite cutting lately about my being a monitor!'

'Oh, that's just his usual teasing, Elizabeth! The reason he's so cool is because you're being nice to Patrick. You know how those two cousins hate each other!'

'But you don't understand, Joan. He thinks I'm being nice to Patrick only because I am a monitor!'

THE NAUGHTIEST GIRL MARCHES ON

Is this a bad attack of the goody-goody-monitor-itis disease? he'd asked her.

'I see,' said Joan. Then she looked at her friend in surprise. What did Elizabeth mean by 'only'? What other reason could she have for being especially nice to Patrick? 'Perhaps you've been overdoing it, Elizabeth. I do believe Julian's a little jealous.'

Elizabeth rapidly changed the subject. It was more than she could bear to think of Julian being her enemy; far worse, even, than it being Daniel.

'We're being silly, Joan,' she declared. 'It couldn't possibly be Julian! Or Daniel, come to that. Let's think of some other people.'

After a while the two girls came to the most obvious conclusion. The message writer was probably one of the gang of boys who admired Jake. Martin, or Kenneth, or John McTavish . . .

'They're probably all in it together,' decided Joan.

But Elizabeth didn't find that any comfort either.

In the distance the bell went for afternoon lessons. As the two girls got to their feet and walked slowly back to school, Elizabeth looked thoughtful.

'Perhaps it doesn't matter who's writing the messages, Joan,' she sighed. 'The fact is I've made a mess of being a monitor. I shouldn't have told tales on Jake. And I shouldn't have allowed myself to get wound up and tried to stop the boys' pillow fights in the way I did. I'm no use as a monitor, if half the boys in the class don't respect me. Perhaps I'd *better* do as the note suggests. Offer to resign.'

'You can't do that, Elizabeth,' said Joan, giving her a sidelong glance. 'You can't give in to anonymous messages.'

'I'm in disgrace anyway,' the naughtiest girl pointed out. 'Don't forget that Thomas is going to deal with me at the next MM! That's what Mr Leslie said. I may have no choice in the matter. I may be asked to resign anyway!'

It was a horrid thought.

'We will just have to see about that, Elizabeth,' replied Joan kindly. 'Won't we?'

In spite of her own troubles Elizabeth began to feel very worried over the next few days about a member of her class.

She had a growing sense of there being something seriously wrong with Jake.

Nobody else noticed much, but Elizabeth found herself keeping a watchful eye on him. She was sure it was connected with the forthcoming hockey match against Milford Grange. She believed he might be dreading it with a sickening fear.

At first she thought it was her imagination, her own

guilty conscience at work. But as each day passed, and the match drew inexorably nearer, she was sure that the big boy was becoming more and more desperate.

'Why don't you want to talk about the big match, Jake?' she heard his friend Kenneth ask him peevishly. 'Why aren't you bothering to practise?'

'My hockey stick will have to do the talking,' Jake had snapped in reply. 'When it needs to!'

He seemed to be avoiding the other boys and they tactfully left him alone.

'He seems a bit tense about the match,' Martin commented. 'I suppose it's because he hasn't played since last season.'

'Jake? Tense about a hockey match?' scoffed John. 'It's schoolwork getting him down, I expect!'

On Friday evening, at the school Meeting, Elizabeth watched Jake from her vantage point on the platform. She thought how glum he looked, wrapped up in his own thoughts. He seemed to take no interest at all when the head boy and girl dealt with the matter of the pillow fights in Room Seventeen.

'As the culprits have owned up, we've decided to let them off lightly,' announced Thomas, while Emma wrote it all down in the school's big Book. 'They must sleep without pillows for a whole week. That will help them to remember that it is thoughtless to keep other boys awake at night! After next week their pillows will be returned to them.'

Even as Elizabeth sat there, wondering what her own punishment was going to be at next week's MM, she noticed that Jake had suddenly gone very pale.

'Finally, we hope you will all turn out and cheer the school hockey team tomorrow morning,' Thomas was saying. 'Milford Grange will be here at eleven o'clock and they are bringing two coachloads of supporters. I am sure you will all be very pleased to know that Jake is fully fit again and is now back in the Whyteleafe team. We are sure he plans to shoot plenty of goals for us tomorrow! Right, everyone. You are dismissed.'

There was laughter and cheers and the sound of benches scraping back. The Meeting was over! The boys and girls were all looking forward to the weekend.

Watching closely, Elizabeth saw Jake rise to his feet and sway slightly. She thought for a moment that he was going to faint. Then he hurried from the hall.

Jake is terrified of tomorrow's match! she realised. *I'm positive now. The very thought of it seems to be making him ill. And it's all my fault! I'm the person who's put him in this position. I think I may have done a dreadful thing!*

Elizabeth hurried down off the platform. Her heart was beating fast. She could not begin to understand what was wrong with Jake, nor why he had been going to such extraordinary lengths to get out of playing hockey for Whyteleafe. But she was racked with guilt to see his suffering.

I've got to catch up with him and tell him how sorry I am! she decided. *I don't care how rude he is to me, I've got to tell him I'm sorry and ask him to forgive me. Oh, what is wrong with him? I do wish there was some way I could make him feel better!*

She raced outside on to the lawn, just in time to see Jake disappearing in the direction of the school gardens. She hurried in pursuit.

When she got there, she saw him sitting quite alone on the wooden bench by the big greenhouse.

The gardens were silent and very still, with no breath of wind today. The rows of runner beans stood like withered green wigwams, their crop near its end. A blackbird rustled in the nearby yew hedge.

Elizabeth's warm heart ached with pity to see the big boy sitting on the bench, doubled up as though in pain. She tiptoed towards him. He was making little moaning sounds.

'Jake!' she whispered.

He raised his head. His eyes looked red.

'Elizabeth!' he gasped in surprise. 'What are you doing here? Please go away. I have such terrible stomach cramps. I can't bear anyone to see me like this.

Please go away – and don't tell anybody you've seen me in such a state!'

'I will *not* go away, Jake!' Elizabeth came and sat beside him and placed an arm round his big shoulders. 'I have come to ask your forgiveness. I know I have done something terrible, giving you away. And now you are scared to play in the match tomorrow. *I* can't bear it to see how scared you are.'

'You've guessed?' asked Jake in alarm.

He buried his face in his hands. Elizabeth patted his heaving back, trying to soothe him.

'I can't bear it that a girl should see me like this,' he moaned.

Elizabeth continued to pat his back gently.

'Please tell me what's wrong, Jake,' she begged. 'I promise on my honour that I'll keep your secret. But I'm so worried about you. I will cry *myself* if you don't tell me what's wrong!'

'I am so very, very scared, Elizabeth,' the boy blurted out. 'I am so frightened that the same thing could happen again.'

'What, Jake?' she prompted him gently, almost in tears herself.

He raised his head and gazed at her. He saw the anguished expression on her face and knew that, in this moment, she was living through his anguish with him. What a fine girl she was, he realised. He suddenly felt sure that he could trust her.

'A month ago, Elizabeth, I nearly blinded somebody,' he stated. 'The person I admire most in all the world. My coach, Henry Hill. Since my father died, he has been like a dad to me! He used to play hockey for England and he's coached me since I was a little boy. But I nearly blinded him. It was touch and go! He's only just come out of hospital.'

'What a terrible thing to happen!' gasped Elizabeth. 'Jake, please tell me the whole story. It will make you feel a little better to talk about it, even if it's only to me.'

At last Jake's strange behaviour began to make sense as he explained that, on the last day of the summer holidays, he'd played in a match for his hometown hockey club. The club's non-playing captain was Henry Hill, a former England international, the man whom Jake so loved and admired. He had coached Jake for years, convinced that the boy would himself play for his country one day. His own playing days were over but, because the team was one short that day, Henry had stepped in at short notice to fill the gap.

It had been a dramatic and closely fought contest, but then had come disaster. A hard-struck ball by Jake had flown off at an angle and the ball had caught Henry in the eye with great force. An ambulance had been called and he'd been rushed to hospital. Only an emergency operation had saved the sight in his left eye.

'It was the most terrible day of my life,' Jake confessed. 'I will never be able to forget it. Henry's cries of pain . . . the ambulance wailing . . . then waiting all afternoon for some news from the hospital . . . I still have bad dreams about it. I really *did* hurt my ankle that day. It was just a slight sprain and my mother bandaged it up for me. Then, when I got back to school, it gave me an idea. I desperately wanted to give myself time! To try to get over what had happened . . .'

'And you didn't want to explain things to Mr Warlow then?' ventured Elizabeth.

'No! He would have told me to put this behind me! He would have tried to rush me. And now I *have* been rushed and the terrible thing is that I *can't* put this behind me, Elizabeth. I will never put it behind me! It is cowardly of me, but I have completely lost my nerve. It could happen again, at any time! It could be something worse next time. Please don't tell anybody about this, Elizabeth. You are the only person who need ever know what a coward I am. I will have to find some new excuse, but . . .'

He buried his face in his hands again. 'I can't play in tomorrow's match. I just can't.'

Elizabeth touched his arm.

'You *must*, Jake,' she whispered. 'You really must, you know. There's somebody you haven't been thinking about in all this.'

He looked at her in surprise. 'Who?'

'Henry, of course. You say he has coached you all this time and believes you will play for your country one day. The accident was a terrible thing, but a younger person would have been able to react more quickly and dodge that flying ball. Henry shouldn't have been playing! But now, having given him one kind of pain, you are planning to make it much worse. You have been his life's work and now you are going to destroy all his dreams for you.'

Jake fell silent. 'I hadn't looked at it like that,' he said at last.

Elizabeth remembered the time that she had fallen badly from her pony. Her governess had forced her instantly to remount. *The longer you leave it, Elizabeth, the more frightened you will be*, she had told the little girl.

'You must play tomorrow, Jake,' she pleaded. 'For Henry's sake you must try to overcome your fears as quickly as possible and get back to playing a hard match once again. Please promise that you will try to overcome your terror.'

'I can't promise, Elizabeth,' Jake said in despair. 'I am so very, very scared about it. Let me just sit here on my own for a while and think things over.'

'Yes, Jake.' Elizabeth rose to her feet. 'And your secret is safe with me. But will you at least promise me something else?'

'What's that, Elizabeth?'

'Ask if you can use the school telephone this evening! Telephone your coach – he'd be pleased to hear from you. And ask his opinion about what he thinks you should do.'

Leaving Jake deep in thought, she tiptoed away.

And the following morning Jake did, indeed, turn out for the match against Milford Grange. His jaw was clenched and his face pale as he ran out on to the pitch with the rest of the Whyteleafe first eleven.

Two people cheered him even louder than the rest. One of them was Elizabeth. The other was a man on the opposite side of the field who had just arrived with his wife. He had a large dressing over one eye, held securely in place by special bandages.

'That's my boy, Jake!' he called out loudly, raising both fists high.

After last night's telephone call Henry Hill had asked his wife to drive him the thirty miles from their home town, so that he could watch Jake's match.

Jake made a nervous, even tentative start, but as the pace hotted up he began to get into his stride. He ran here, there and everywhere, tackling fiercely, soon caught up in the excitement of the hard-fought game. By the end of the match, Whyteleafe had won 6–4 and Jake had scored five of the six goals!

As he walked off the pitch, Henry Hill came striding across to shake his hand.

'That was marvellous, Jake.' His face was shining and so was Jake's. 'I'm very proud of you, my boy. Keep it up. What a tonic for a poor, sick invalid!'

'I've got to drag Henry away, Jake,' apologised Mrs Hill, tugging at her husband's arm. 'We're due at the hospital. The bandages come off today. Isn't that good news? I'm hoping the dear man has seen sense at last. I've told him to face the fact that his glory days are behind him. I hope that's going to be his last game!'

'It is. It is. But Jake's got all his glory days ahead of him. I'm so proud of you, my boy!' the man repeated, as he pumped Jake's hand and slapped him on the back. 'Good luck! See you at half-term!'

Jake watched his coach walk away. He was overcome with emotion.

Some of his classmates came racing over then and tried to close in on him. Martin, Kenneth, John . . . they were all very excited.

'Was that your famous coach, Jake?'

'Was that Henry Hill?'

But Jake strode away from them.

'Where's Elizabeth?' he demanded. 'Where's our famous monitor? That's who I want to see right now.'

To everybody's surprise, when he found Elizabeth, he lifted her clean off the ground and swung her up on to his shoulders.

'Thank you, Elizabeth! You're the best monitor in the school! If anybody says any different, tell them to come and see me!'

The second-form boys all looked at one another in amazement.

'What's Elizabeth done then?' asked Kenneth.

'Given me my nerve back, that's what she's done!' Jake informed them. He was not ashamed to admit it to anyone now. 'I'll tell you the whole story later!'

Julian and Joan were surprised to see Jake parading round the hockey pitch with Elizabeth perched up high on his shoulders. He wanted her to share in his glory. She was laughing and waving to everybody. Some of the boys were cheering her!

'What's the naughtiest girl been up to now?' wondered Julian.

The story of how Elizabeth had helped Jake soon spread round the school. There were no more anonymous messages after that.

But the Monitors' Meeting still lay ahead.

CHAPTER TEN

A MYSTERY STILL UNSOLVED

'IT WAS a reckless thing to do, Elizabeth. You had no business charging into the boys' quarters at night and encouraging some of your friends to join you! You must have known you were breaking a strict school rule,' said Thomas. 'That is hardly a sensible way for a monitor to deal with others who are breaking rules. By breaking one herself!'

The next MM was taking place. Silent and ashamed, Elizabeth sat next to Joan on the bench in the cosy little study. The moment of reckoning had come at last, the moment she had been dreading.

'You will never live down your naughtiest girl nickname if you do things like this, Elizabeth,' Emma pointed out. 'Because you are a monitor, we have spared you the shame of discussing this at the weekly Meeting. But it cannot go unpunished.'

'We understand that you were provoked,' went on Thomas, as the rest of the monitors listened with interest. 'Joan has told us that you were being teased and receiving anonymous messages from boys who appeared to think it unfair that your class has two girl monitors. They should have thought of that before, when they held the election! So Emma and I have decided on quite a modest punishment. You and your four friends must all go to bed one hour earlier for the next seven days. Do the other monitors think that sounds fair?'

There were murmurs of agreement from everyone. They all liked the naughtiest girl. She did crazy things sometimes, but she had a very warm heart. They had all heard the story about Jake by now.

How marvellous that Joan had been and spoken up for her, thought Elizabeth. She felt herself going weak at the knees. She had got off lightly! What a relief! And what a relief it would be to give the good news to Jenny, Kathleen, Belinda and Tessa. She had felt guilty about leading them into trouble. She was sure they would not mind having to go to bed early for a few nights, any more than she did.

But, just as her heart began to lighten, Emma spoke again.

'However, this whole situation has raised an

important issue. Tom and I have had a long talk about it and we've talked it over with Joan, too. There are a lot of boys in Form Two. We feel that perhaps a mistake was made in appointing two girl monitors. What do you think, Elizabeth?'

'I – I—'

Elizabeth's spirits plunged. So she was going to be asked to resign after all!

'If the form had had a boy monitor in office, some problems might have been avoided,' Thomas observed. 'For example, Jake is a big boy who prides himself on his physical strength. It was extremely difficult for him to confess to a girl how very frightened he felt. He might have found it easier to talk to another boy. It's just possible.'

'Yes,' agreed Elizabeth. She steeled herself. 'If you want me to stand down, then I will quite understand . . .'

'Oh, Elizabeth, of course not!' exclaimed Joan. 'Not you – me!'

'Yes, cheer up, Elizabeth!' smiled Emma. 'Joan has already offered us her resignation. She feels that she has had a very long stint as monitor, whereas you have only just started. Even more important, she is finding that being a monitor is starting to clash with her swimming commitments. She has assured me that she will be perfectly happy to make way for a boy and she believes this is necessary.'

'Joan!' whispered Elizabeth in surprise. 'Is this true? And is it true that you are going to be quite happy about it?'

'Perfectly true!' replied her friend. 'And perfectly happy!'

After further discussion it was agreed that Joan would stand down as monitor at the end of the next School Meeting. And after that the second-form boys could elect a monitor from among their number in time for the last Meeting before half-term.

Towards the end of the MM, the head boy and girl asked anxiously if any more citations had been handed in for the William and Rita Award.

There were three this week.

They all agreed that one of them was outstanding and should go on the shortlist. Elizabeth was very pleased about that. For it was one that Elizabeth herself had written out on the special form. Joan had read it beautifully.

'Won't it be lovely if our citation wins the award, Joan?' she said, as they walked into tea together. 'What an honour for the second form!'

'What's that?' asked Patrick in alarm, for he was just behind them.

'Don't worry, Patrick!' Elizabeth turned round and

smiled at him. 'You shouldn't eavesdrop. But you can relax now. Something else has come up, so you're quite safe!'

'Whatever was that about?' asked Joan, looking puzzled as she watched Patrick stroll on past them, whistling softly.

'Oh, nothing, Joan,' Elizabeth replied quickly.

She smiled to herself. Dear Patrick. He could sleep easily in his bed at nights. Perhaps one day she would be able to persuade him to be nominated, in time for a future award. But there was no hurry now.

She was so pleased that she was going to be able to continue as a monitor. Joan really did not want to be one any more. But she was going to miss her. It had been so wonderful having a best friend as the other monitor, somebody to talk over the MMs with, to their heart's content. Who would the new monitor be? she wondered. Who would the boys elect? She would find out soon enough. She hoped it would be somebody she liked.

The one small irritation was the matter of those anonymous messages. The person who'd written them had in part got his way! Although he'd not succeeded in getting rid of Elizabeth as a monitor, there *was* going to be a boy monitor, which would no doubt please him. It was annoying to think of her enemy being pleased.

A MYSTERY STILL UNSOLVED

Who had written the notes? Would she ever find out?

It was a mystery still unsolved.

CHAPTER ELEVEN

JULIAN SPRINGS A HUGE SURPRISE

TRUTH WILL always out and the truth about the enemy came out in an amazing way. It was the last person that Elizabeth suspected. It came out at the next Meeting.

All the usual weekly business had been conducted. And then Emma announced that Joan would be resigning as a monitor.

'There are a lot of boys in the second form this year. It has been decided by all concerned that it would be better to have one boy and one girl monitor. We shall be asking the second-form boys to elect their representative at next week's Meeting, ready for the second half of term. In the meantime could we all give Joan a round of applause, please, for her long and distinguished service to the second form.'

There was prolonged applause for Joan. Some of the boys and girls cheered and stamped their feet as well.

JULIAN SPRINGS A HUGE SURPRISE

Sitting proudly next to her on the platform, Elizabeth glanced at her friend affectionately. How she was going to miss the great adventure of their being monitors together! But Joan had set her heart on getting strong and fit enough to be a member of Miss Thomas's swimming team and her time was going to be rationed now.

As the applause died away, the children all started chattering. They thought that the Meeting was over. But Thomas rapped the table sharply with the little gavel.

'Silence, please. There is one more matter to attend to. I'll let Emma do the talking.'

The head girl stood up.

'Somewhere in this hall there is a boy who broke a school rule and went to the village on his own, two or three weeks ago,' she stated. 'It was very wrong of him for the rule is a very strict one. But just this once he will not be punished. I can see you are all wondering why,' she added, for a great hush had fallen over the hall. 'Well, I can tell you why. A woman has been to see us today. She brought this with her.'

Lying on the table, next to the school Book, was a large cardboard box. Emma took something out of the box. With a dramatic flourish she held it up for the whole school to see.

THE NAUGHTIEST GIRL MARCHES ON

It was a giant box of chocolates.

All the children gasped with excitement. What was coming next? Elizabeth stiffened. She stared down into the hall to the second-form benches. Patrick was sitting there, a slow pallor creeping up his cheeks.

'With no thought of danger to himself this boy rushed into the road and saved the woman's child from being run over. The child was walking straight into the path of an oncoming car and would no doubt have been injured – or worse – without this boy's intervention. However, he hurried away without waiting to be thanked.'

Emma paused for breath.

'After that, the woman saw the boy on a more recent occasion. The child recognised him at once. On this occasion the mother managed quickly to thank him, but once again he hurried off. She feels he deserves some proper reward and she has asked that he be presented with this box of chocolates in front of the whole school. So Thomas and I would now like our shy hero to stand up and make himself known. Who is he, please?'

The pupils were enthralled. They started whispering and nudging one another, gazing all round the hall. Who would stand up?

Elizabeth was staring at Patrick in deep fascination. What was going to happen now? In spite of all his efforts to keep his heroism a secret it was going to be impossible for him to hide it now!

Patrick seemed to be frozen to the bench. His eyes were darting this way and that. Once or twice he craned his neck to look round at the benches behind him.

He's still trying to keep it secret, even now! thought Elizabeth. *He's looking around, like everybody else. Pretending that he's waiting to see who's going to stand up.*

Emma stood there, holding the chocolates. The seconds ticked by. And Patrick still sat there, gazing all around. Two or three places along on the bench, Julian scratched his head and looked puzzled. Other children were talking in low voices. It was beginning to get embarrassing.

'Would the boy please stand up?' repeated Emma, colouring a little.

Still no one did so. Then Thomas lost patience. He banged the gavel hard on the table.

'Would the boy in question stand up at once, please?' he said. 'That's an order.'

Elizabeth managed to catch Patrick's eye. And then slowly, very slowly, Patrick rose to his feet, his face drained of colour. But then Elizabeth gave a little gasp. For something very strange was happening. At exactly the same moment Julian was slowly rising too! Languidly, his hands in his pockets.

107

Both boys were standing up together!

'Was this child a girl and did she have red hair by any chance?' enquired Julian.

'Yes, she was a girl. And her mother certainly has red hair,' replied Thomas. 'Why, do you know something about it? Please take your hands out of your pockets, Julian.'

With Patrick now standing frozen in horror, a little further along the same bench, Julian took his hands out of his pockets and grinned.

'I think it must have been me then. I'm afraid I'd forgotten all about it. What perplexed me was Emma saying the boy was seen in the village a second time. You see I haven't been down again since the other week when that kid ran in the road! But now I realise –' he turned and smiled at Patrick with a scornful gleam in his eye – 'that she could have confused me with somebody else.'

Patrick looked as though he wished the ground would swallow him up. Slowly, he subsided back down on to the bench.

Elizabeth gazed from one cousin to the other in shock. She was reminded how alike they looked, with their matted black hair and brilliant green eyes! How easy it would have been for the child to make her mistake!

JULIAN SPRINGS A HUGE SURPRISE

It was not Patrick who'd performed the brave deed at all. It was Julian! And now Julian was strolling up to the platform and being presented with the chocolates! And the whole school was clapping and cheering him! Meanwhile, down below, Patrick sat miserably hunched on the bench.

And, when all the excitement had died down, Thomas held his hand up for silence one last time. He asked Patrick to get to his feet.

'Don't ever try to do that again,' he told him, shaming him in front of the whole school. 'Of all the kinds of stealing there are, to try to steal another person's glory is the most despicable.'

The head boy was angry enough, but Elizabeth's own anger put even his in the shade. She could hardly wait to vent her feelings.

'You complete and absolute worm!' she told Patrick afterwards, dragging him outside on to the terrace. 'No wonder you didn't want me to name you for the William and Rita Award! If I'd done that, the person who had really performed the brave deed would soon have had something to say about it, wouldn't they? How could you bear to let me think you were a hero all this time? You have made an absolute fool of me. I hate you!'

'Please don't hate me, Elizabeth,' begged Patrick.

'You never gave me the chance to explain that the little girl had made a mistake. You really didn't! I had no idea who'd really saved her. I hadn't a clue. But it was just so thrilling to have you looking up to me and liking me for a change! I would have explained straight away, but you never gave me the chance, Elizabeth! And after that I thought, what harm could it possibly do anyone else, the child making a silly mistake and you thinking it was me?'

Elizabeth's anger began to subside as she saw how distressed the boy was. She also realised that he was telling the truth. She'd given him almost no chance at all to explain there'd been a mistake! She'd made such a fuss of him at the time. It must have been awkward for him.

'It all seemed so simple at first,' Patrick confessed. 'It was so nice that you liked me. And the woman seemed really pleased to have someone to thank! I thought nothing more would come of it. But then it was dreadful when this business of the award came up and you wanted to put my name forward! I longed to make a clean breast of things but, when you told me that you'd given up your place in the table-tennis team, I was finished! That was the worst thing of all, Elizabeth. After that I became desperate that the truth should never, ever come out. I even wrote those silly notes—'

'*You* wrote the notes, Patrick?' gasped Elizabeth. '*You* were the enemy? I thought of everyone else, but I never thought of you!'

'I'm not an enemy, Elizabeth. But I knew that as long as you kept on going to those MMs of yours, sooner or later you'd have blurted something out about my so-called brave deed. I know what you're like! So I was hoping, with some of the boys making trouble for you anyway, that you might get fed up with being a monitor.'

'I see.'

Elizabeth frowned. She didn't know whether to be angry or amused. For she was relieved to discover that she did not have a real enemy.

'Patrick, I think you are pathetic!' she added.

'Well, I really *did* think it was unfair having two girl monitors,' Patrick objected. 'I've always said that.'

Elizabeth thought back over all the time she'd known Patrick.

It was true! He had often said it. In fact, he didn't really approve of the school having girls in it at all! How silly of her not to have remembered that.

'Well, there's going to be a boy monitor anyway,' she pointed out.

'Yes,' replied Patrick smugly. 'Thomas and Emma seem to agree with me on that.'

Elizabeth turned on her heel. Julian had appeared on the terrace, looking for her. She called back to Patrick, over her shoulder.

'I only hope it's not you, Patrick!'

Julian grinned. 'Hello, Elizabeth. Been giving my cousin a telling-off about something? Here, have a chocolate. They're delicious.'

It was the last Meeting before half-term. A gleaming little silver trophy stood on the head boy and girl's table. The very first William and Rita Award was about to be announced.

'We ended up with four citations on the shortlist,' Thomas was telling the assembled school, 'of which two were quite outstanding. Miss Belle and Miss Best and Emma and I had a very difficult job deciding between them. One was for Julian Holland, signed by several boys in his class, for his brave action in saving the little girl from being run over. The other was for Jake Johnson, signed by Elizabeth Allen, for his courage in overcoming a personal crisis.'

While the whole school hung on to his words Thomas paused for maximum effect.

'Which one were we to choose? Which boy had shown the greater courage? As we talked it over, we came to realise that Julian's fearless deed had come as second nature to him. It was truly fearless for he had felt no fear. He saw the child in danger and instantly took action. We are very proud of him for that. But his brave deed meant so little to him that he had some difficulty in remembering it afterwards.

'Jake, on the other hand, and I know he does not mind us telling you this now, felt absolute terror at the thought of playing hockey again after inflicting a grave injury on someone he loved and admired. Yet somehow he faced that fear and fought it and, in the end, he overcame it.

'Fearlessness and courage are not the same thing. A high form of courage is to know real fear – and then to overcome it. The school therefore takes great pride in giving the very first William and Rita Award to – Jake Johnson.'

The school clapped and cheered as the gentle giant of a boy shambled up on the platform and took the little silver trophy from Emma's outstretched hand. He clutched it proudly and shot Elizabeth an embarrassed smile. She was sitting behind Emma on the platform, clapping so hard that her palms stung.

As the Meeting broke up, she turned to the boy sitting next to her.

'A lot of the boys wanted you to have the award, Julian, but I think the Beauty and the Beast and Thomas and Emma have all made the right decision, don't you?'

'Most definitely,' agreed Julian.

'And at least the boys elected you as monitor!' she said, with a happy sigh.

It was nice to have Julian sitting next to her on the platform.

She would still have a friend as her fellow monitor after all. A truly marvellous friend. Poor Patrick! But what fun it was going to be from now on, she and Julian being monitors together!

'Yes, I'm a monitor,' replied Julian, with a cheerful grin. 'I still can't believe it and, as a matter of fact, Elizabeth, I don't know how I'm going to manage it. But for your sake I suppose I'd better try.'

'You suppose right, Julian,' she laughed.

BONUS BLYTON

Enid Blyton has been one of the world's best-loved storytellers for over seventy years. Her interest in writing began as a child and before she loved receiving letters from the children who read her books, she enjoyed working with them as a teacher. The Naughtiest Girl stories are inspired by real schools and experiences. Turn the page to learn more about Enid as a child and as a teacher. Afterwards you might like to write about your school and teachers and the people in *your* class!

THE LIFE AND TIMES OF
ENID BLYTON

11 August 1897	Enid Blyton was born in East Dulwich, London. Two brothers are born after her – Hanly (b. 1899) and Carey (b. 1902).
1911	Enid enters a children's poetry competition and is praised for her writing. She's on the path to becoming a bestselling author . . .
1916	Enid begins to train as a teacher in Ipswich. By the time she is 21, she is a fully qualified Froebel teacher, and starts work at a school in Kent.
1917	Enid's first 'grown-up' publication – three poems in *Nash's Magazine*.
June 1922	Enid's first book is published. It's called *Child Whispers*.
1926	Enid begins editing – and writes – the phenomenal *Sunny Stories for Little Folks* magazine. (She continues in this role for 26 years!)

1927	So vast is Enid's output that she has to learn to type. (But she still writes to children by hand.)
1931	Having married Hugh Pollock in 1924, the couple's first child, Gillian, is born. Imogen, their second daughter, was born in 1935.
1942	The Famous Five is launched with *Five on a Treasure Island*.
1949	The first appearance of *The Secret Seven* and of *Noddy* mark this year as special.
1953	Enid moves away from *Sunny Stories* to launch *Enid Blyton's Magazine*. She is now renowned throughout the world – she even established her own company, called Darrell Waters Limited (the surname of her second husband).
1962	Enid Blyton becomes one of the first and most important children's authors to be published in paperback. Now she reaches even more readers than ever before.
28 November 1968	Enid dies in her sleep, in a nursing home in Hampstead.

SCHOOL RULES

Elizabeth is used to getting her own way, so it's a challenge to adapt to life at Whyteleafe where the students make their own rules. That said, the student council don't have many rules at all. Here are the ones explained to the new children in *The Naughtiest Girl in the School* . . .

'We place all the money we get into this box, and we draw from it two shillings a week each. The rest of the money is used to buy anything that any of you especially want – but you have to state at the weekly Meeting what you need the money for, and the Jury will decide if you may have it.

'The second rule is that if we have any complaint at all, we must bring it to the Meeting and announce it there, so that everyone may hear it, and decide what is to be done with it. Please be sure you understand the difference between a real complaint and telling tales, because telling tales is also punished.'

In that first book in the series we learn that 'monitors are chosen for their common sense, their loyalty to the school and its ideas, and their good character. They must be obeyed, because you yourselves have chosen them'.

MY HAPPIEST TIMES

During her lifetime, Enid Blyton received many hundreds of letters from the thousands of children – all over the world – who enjoyed reading her books. She took great pleasure in replying to them. She also loved meeting children and it is said that the suggestion for an autobiography came from a young fan who presented Enid with a list of questions. He thought he might write a book about his favourite author, called *Enid Blyton – The Story of Her Life*, but his mother suggested that Enid might write it herself. And so she did. *The Story of My Life* was published in 1952. Enid wrote about her family, where she lived, the inspiration for her books and her writing process. She also talked about her childhood. Have you ever imagined what your favourite writers were like as children – and what important events may have shaped their future lives? Here is an extract from *The Story of My Life*, which takes us back to Enid's younger days . . .

* * *

My happiest childhood times were when I was reading and dreaming, when I was playing games with other children, and when I was out in the country or by the sea. Very much like your happiest times, I expect!

The games I played were Burglars and Police Officers, Making a House somewhere – behind a bush, or up a tree, or under a table. We had tops and hoops and marbles as the seasons came round.

We played a great many card games, because we all loved cards. So do my own girls. We played Snap and Happy Families, Old Maid and Beggar-My-Neighbour.

We also played board games such as Snakes and Ladders (and sometimes Ladders and Snakes – going up the snakes and down the ladders, instead of the other way round!). When I was six, my father taught me to play draughts and a little later he taught me to play chess. That was just before I was seven. He thought that all young children should learn to play chess. I enjoyed the games immensely.

I think my father was more of a naturalist than anything else. I didn't even know what a naturalist was at that time – all I knew was that my father loved the countryside, loved flowers and birds and wild animals, and knew more about them than anyone I had ever met. And what was more he was willing to take me with him on his expeditions, and share his love and his knowledge with me!

In those days it was considered quite ordinary to collect birds' eggs. Nowadays we teach children not to, because it distresses the birds and it might lead to many kinds gradually becoming extinct.

My father collected birds' eggs, and he had a cabinet of little drawers full of beautiful eggs, neatly arranged and labelled. One of the things I had to do to help him was to insert my hand into holes in trees to see if any nests were there, and to feel for eggs.

I never did like taking the eggs. I did so hope the bird wouldn't mind. Fortunately my father never wanted more than one egg. He never knew how scared I was of putting my hand down into those small holes. Once I heard a hissing noise down a hole, and I was sure it was an adder hiding there. I was afraid of being bitten, but I didn't like to say so.

Weekend after weekend I went out with my father. Looking back, it seems as if those days were always warm, always sunny, and that the sky was always as deeply blue as the cornflowers in my garden, or as faintly blue as the harebells on the common.

We were lucky to have woods and commons, ponds and lanes so near. We explored everywhere and everything – watching the lizards play on the sunny banks, listening to the willow warblers singing, poking down a hole that my father said badgers had been in, looking for the white violets we knew always blossomed in a certain dell.

All my childhood was steeped in the sunshine of the woods and commons and lanes, and what I didn't find out from nature herself I read about in books, and then searched for it again. I was perfectly happy, even when I wandered about alone, finding flowers to look up in our reference books, trying to discover what bird was singing, learning the difference between a thrush's nest and a blackbird's, and a hundred other things.

'One day I'll put all these things into a book,' I said, though I didn't tell anyone that, of course.

WHAT THEY DID AT
MISS BROWN'S SCHOOL

In 1920 Enid Blyton became a governess to the four Thompson children, whose ages ranged from four to ten. The family lived in Surbiton, in Surrey, in a house called 'Southernhay'. Enid had a small room which overlooked the garden, and it was there that she wrote many of her stories. Enid's tiny class often had lessons outdoors in the summer months.

Enid was very popular with her students, because her lessons were both practical and creative. She worked with them to put on performances for which they made props, costumes and invitations – and even sold tickets.

In 1941 she published a long story called 'What They Did at Miss Brown's School', which was divided into monthly episodes. It's been hard to find for many years, but you can read extracts in these new editions of *The Naughtiest Girl* books. The character of Miss Brown and her tiny class is very much based on Enid Blyton and her school at the Thompsons' . . .

Here's the eleventh extract . . .

11. November. Getting to Know the Birds

THERE WAS no doubt at all what the 'special thing' was to be for November! It was to be a bird table, of course, and all the children meant to bring something for it every day.

John made the table, and he made it very well. He brought an old post to school and dug a hole for it not far from the classroom. He set the post in the hole, filled in the earth and got everyone to stamp it down firmly. Then he brought a broad, flat piece of wood, on to which he had nailed an upright edge or rim around three sides.

'Why haven't you put a rim to the front edge, John?' asked Peter.

'So that we can clean the dirt easily off the table,' said John. 'I've put the rim on to keep our food from blowing off – but from one side we shall want to scrape off the old food and dirt.'

'You have made it nicely, John,' Susan cried, hopping

round it on one foot.

'Susan thinks she's a bird hopping about for food already!' laughed Mary. John hammered the tabletop on to the post. Soon it was fixed and the bird table was ready. It really was a very simple thing to make.

'And now we must each of us bring scraps and crumbs every day for the table,' said Mary. 'Can we take it in turns to clean the table and put out fresh water, Miss Brown?'

'Yes. Take a week each,' said Miss Brown. 'John can begin, as he is the eldest.'

Well, it *was* fun, having the bird table! All day long the birds were on it, either eating the food or waiting for it, or drinking the water or bathing in it! The children saw their little feathered friends every time they looked up from their books.

Each morning all kinds of scraps were put on the table. The children packed them into old ice-cream tubs or cartons, and brought them along.

'I've got rice-pudding scrapings!' cried Susan.

'And I've got soaked dog biscuits from my dog's dish!' said John.

'And I've got potato, a bone and breadcrumbs!' said Mary.

'And I've got some bacon rind!' said Peter.

'What a feast for the birds!' said Miss Brown, giving

John the crumbs from her table. 'No wonder they come all day long! We must make a bird chart, I think.'

So they made a bird chart, and put on it each bird that came to their bird table, and the things that every bird ate.

Sparrows, chaffinches, starlings, tits, hedge sparrows, blackbirds, thrushes, robins, wrens and wagtails visited the table. Each child looked for pictures of these birds in papers or magazines, and cut them out when they found them. Then the pictures were coloured correctly and pasted on the chart. The children put down the names of the birds and what kinds of things they ate. It was great fun.

They put a sunflower head on the table and that day they had a new visitor – a greenfinch with a pretty gold bar on its wing! It did love the sunflower seeds.

'Another bird for our chart!' said John in glee.

Then Peter brought a coconut and said he wanted to give it to the tits. So Miss Brown knocked a hole in each end and hung it up on a piece of string just outside the classroom window. The tits were on it all day long.

'Now we can easily learn the difference between the three tits!' said Mary, pleased. 'Great tit is the biggest and brightest, with its black head and green and yellow dress. Blue tit is the prettiest, with its blue cap and small body – and coal tit is the tiniest, with his black head, dull colouring and white streak down the back of its head!'

'Very good, Mary!' said Miss Brown, pleased. 'You are using your eyes well!'

The children became most interested in their birds, and longed to do more for them. So Miss Brown took them shopping one day, and they brought a bag of hemp seed, which the birds love, some brazil nuts and some peanuts.

'The hemp seed is a favourite of the seed-eating birds such as the sparrows and finches,' said Miss Brown. 'The peanuts and the brazil nuts will be enjoyed by the tits. They love all nuts.'

Miss Brown cracked the brazil nuts and tied each one on to a separate bit of string. Then she hung the nuts from nails round the bird table on their strings.

The tits soon found them – and how the children laughed to see them hauling up the brazil nuts 'hand over hand like a sailor' as Susan said. They held them firmly in their little feet and pecked away hard.

The children scattered a little hemp seed each day on the table and the hard-billed birds enjoyed it immensely. Sometimes there were as many as twenty or more birds on the table, and there really didn't seem room.

'Let's nail a few twigs to the back of the table, Miss Brown,' said John. 'Then those birds that come last can perch on the twigs and wait for their turn.'

So little branching twigs were nailed to the back of the table, and the birds always perched on these before flying on to the table itself. It was pretty to see them there.

'Now we mustn't forget our peanuts,' said Miss Brown. 'I have bought you a peanut feeder to hang up by the window, children – it will be such fun to watch it!'

She showed them the peanut feeder. It was quite a simple thing – just a cylinder of tin between two wooden pieces, top and bottom. The cylinder of tin had a slit down the middle each side, and through these slits the tits pecked away at the peanuts.

'We must shell the peanuts first, before we slip them into the feeder,' said Miss Brown. So they all shelled hard, and at last the feeder was full. Miss Brown corked up the hole at the bottom, through which she had slipped the nuts, and hung up the feeder just by the window.

In two minutes there were four tits on it – a great tit, two blue tits and a coal tit! How pleased and excited they were! So were the children. They could hardly do their arithmetic because they wanted to watch the tits.

'Miss Brown, I saw a funny wooden sort of bell thing in the seedshop today,' said Mary that afternoon. 'It was called a tit bell. Was it for the tits – and what has to be done to it? It wasn't very much money. I could buy it if you think it would be fun to have.'

'Oh, *yes*, Mary, it would be lovely to have a tit bell,' said Miss Brown. 'If you can afford to buy it, do get it and bring it tomorrow. I will show you how to use it.'

So the next day Mary came along, proudly carrying her tit bell. It was just like a wooden bell, with no clapper inside, of course, but just a tiny perch across the wide end.

'Now we fill this little bell with fat,' said Miss Brown. 'I've got some on my kitchen stove, ready for the bell. Mary, get a cup, and put the bell upside down in it, so that I can easily pour the fat inside.'

Mary stood the bell in a cup and Miss Brown came back with the melted fat. She poured it carefully into the tit bell.

'There!' she said. 'Now, as soon as the fat has set hard, we will hang the bell up by the peanut feeder – what fun! The tits will soon find it and will creep into the bell, hang upside down, and peck out the fat! No other bird can get the fat – though I expect the robin will try to – because, you see, the only birds that are true little acrobats are the tits!'

The fat soon set, and the bell was hung up outside. It wasn't long before a crowd of tits were all trying to get into the bell and peck the fat. They shouted at one another and the blue tits lifted up their little crests and cried '*Chururururrr!*' very angrily indeed.

'I *do* wish I had a tit bell in my garden at home,' sighed Susan. 'I would like to see the tits coming to it all day long.'

'Well, Susan, ask your mother to save you a nice mutton bone,' said Miss Brown. 'Hang it to a branch by a string and the tits will come and peck away at the fat. It will be as good as a tit bell for you!'

'Oh, that's a lovely idea!' said Susan, pleased.

When the children went for their nature walks, they hunted for all kinds of berries and seeds to bring back for their bird table – and what a lot they found! Hips and haws, elderberries, privet berries, yew berries, spindleberries – and so many different kinds of seeds that the birds must have been really astonished at all they had.

Susan brought back some thistles, with downy heads still full of seeds. She asked John to tie them to the twigs at the back of the table for her.

'Who do you think is going to eat thistle seeds?' asked John.

'My mummy says that goldfinches are fond of thistle seeds,' said Susan seriously. 'And we haven't had goldfinches yet, have we? Well, I want them – so I've got these thistles!'

Well, Susan's mother was quite right – the goldfinches *did* love thistledown for the very next day there came not *one* goldfinch, but seven. They alighted on the twigs like a flock of fairy birds, brightly coloured, with plenty of shining yellow gold about them.

The children were too delighted for words. They left their writing and went to the window to watch. Miss Brown came too.

'We call a flock of goldfinches a *charm* of goldfinches,' she said. 'Don't you think it is a good name for such enchanting little birds!'

'*I* am going to put the goldfinches on our bird chart,' said Susan. 'Because it was *my* thistles that brought them here!'

And she found a beautiful coloured picture of a goldfinch and proudly pasted it on the chart. She wrote below the picture: 'This is a goldfinch. For its food it eats my thistledown.'

That made everyone laugh – but Susan didn't care. She was so pleased to have brought the prettiest of the birds to the bird table!

'I'm going to get my daddy to make me a bird table of my own,' she said.

'I've got one already,' said John.

'So have I,' said Mary.

'Well, I shall have one too, like Susan,' said Peter.

'It really is a lovely thing to have, and it's such fun to make friends with the birds like this.'

'I hoped you would all have tables of your own before the year was out!' said Miss Brown, smiling. 'I made up my mind not to suggest it at all, but to see if our own table would give you enough pleasure to make you each want one too. And sure enough it has!'

So after that there were five tables to see to, instead of one, and you will be glad to know that every table was spread with food and fresh water without being once forgotten. Good children, weren't they?

ENIDBLYTON.CO.UK
IS FOR PARENTS, CHILDREN AND TEACHERS!

Sign up to the newsletter on the homepage for a monthly round-up of news from the world of

Enid Blyton

JOIN US ON SOCIAL MEDIA

Enid Blyton

is one of the most popular children's authors of all time. Her books have sold over 500 million copies and have been translated into other languages more often than any other children's author.

Enid Blyton adored writing for children. She wrote over 700 books and about 2,000 short stories. *The Famous Five* books, now 75 years old, are her most popular. She is also the author of other favourites including *The Secret Seven*, *The Magic Faraway Tree*, *Malory Towers* and *Noddy*.

Born in London in 1897, Enid lived much of her life in Buckinghamshire and loved dogs, gardening and the countryside. She was very knowledgeable about trees, flowers, birds and animals.

Dorset – where some of the Famous Five's adventures are set – was a favourite place of hers too.

Enid Blyton's stories are read and loved by millions of children (and grown-ups) all over the world. Visit enidblyton.co.uk to discover more.

Illustration by
Laura Ellen Anderson.